Frogs!

In the center of the village, the full extent of the green plague could now be seen. What had been a trickle of family Ranidae at breakfast had, by lunch, become a tidal wave.

Put simply: There were frogs everywhere.

Some were small green blobs and some were enormous ten-inch-round boulders. They seemed to stretch from the foot of Grossmutter to the foot of Harlingberg, the two mountains that made up the sides of the village's valley.

The children were the only ones who were enjoying the spectacle. They had abandoned their own games of tag and hide-and-seek to start frog racing and frog-jumping contests with the more agreeable frogs.

But as frogs continued to flood into the town, even the children lost interest. A frog or two or seven in the street is one thing. But a frog floating languidly in your milk glass or curled up on your pillow or draped across your toothbrush is another.

—from Jane Yolen's "Green Plague"

· ⌣ ·

"[A] collection full of fun stories that fans of the included authors and amphibiaphiles will definitely enjoy." —*VOYA*

OTHER PUFFIN BOOKS YOU MAY ENJOY

Ribbiting Tales

Ribbiting Tales

Original Stories about Frogs

Edited by
NANCY SPRINGER

Illustrated by
TONY DITERLIZZI

PUFFIN BOOKS

Keone'ula Elementary School

PUFFIN BOOKS
Published by the Penguin Group
Penguin Putnam Books for Young Readers,
345 Hudson Street, New York, New York 10014, U.S.A.
Penguin Books Ltd, 80 Strand , London WC2R ORL, England
Penguin Books Australia Ltd, Ringwood, Victoria, Australia
Penguin Books Canada Ltd, 10 Alcorn Avenue, Toronto, Ontario, Canada M4V 3B2
Penguin Books (N.Z.) Ltd, 182-190 Wairau Road, Auckland 10, New Zealand

Penguin Books Ltd, Registered Offices: Harmondsworth, Middlesex, England

First published in the United States of America by Philomel Books,
a division of Penguin Putnam Books for Young Readers, 2000
Published by Puffin Books,
a division of Penguin Putnam Books for Young Readers, 2002

1 3 5 7 9 10 8 6 4 2

Compilations copyright © Philomel Books, 2000
Illustrations copyright © Tony DiTerlizzi, 2000

"In the Frog King's Court" © Bruce Coville, 2000
"Old Jim Croaker Jumps over the Moon" © Robert J. Harris, 2000
"It Came from Outer Little Pond" © Brian Jacques, 2000
"Delia Broom and the Frog-People of Quicksand Pond" © Janet Taylor Lisle, 2000
"A Boy and His Frog" © David Lubar, 2000
"Polliwog" © Stephen Menick, 2000
"Ahem" © Nancy Springer, 2000
"Green Plague" © Jane Yolen, 2000

All rights reserved

THE LIBRARY OF CONGRESS HAS CATALOGED THE PHILOMEL EDITION AS FOLLOWS:
Ribbiting tales: original stories about frogs / edited by Nancy Springer;
Illustrated by Tony DiTerlizzi.
p. cm.
Summary: An anthology of humorous stories celebrating the slimy frog by
such authors as Robert J. Harris, Brian Jacques, and Jane Yolen
1. Children's stories. 2. Humorous stories. 3. Frogs—Juvenile fiction.
[1. Frogs—Fiction. 2. Humorous stories. 3. Short stories.]
I. Springer, Nancy. II. DiTerlizzi, Tony, ill.
PZ5.R36 2000 [Fic]—dc21 99-055402
ISBN 0-399-23312-1

Puffin Books ISBN 0-698-11952-5

Printed in the United States of America

Except in the United States of America, this book is sold subject to the condition that
it shall not, by way of trade or otherwise, be lent, re-sold, hired out, or otherwise
circulated without the publisher's prior consent in any form of binding or cover
other than that in which it is published and without a similar condition
including this condition being imposed on the subsequent purchaser.

Contents

• • •

Ribbiting Tales

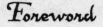

Foreword

• • •

Several years ago, in the public library, I happened across a nonfiction book called *Frogs, Their Wonderful Wisdom, Follies and Foibles, Mysterious Powers, Strange Encounters, Private Lives, Symbolism and Meaning*, edited by Gerald Donaldson. To say that it interested me in frogs would be an understatement. I've been writing novels and stories featuring frogs ever since.

The frog, with its dainty hands, its delicate, hairless skin, its arms and legs, is the most human looking of animals. It's no coincidence that the animal requesting a kiss in the classic fairy tale is a frog prince, not a hedgehog prince. In such tales we see the frog as ourselves, tiny adventurers in a huge, incomprehensible world.

However, the frog, with its wide mouth, its bulging eyes, its muddy green coloring (if it's not even more alien of hue), is also funny looking to the point of being repulsive. If a frog is human looking, then the human it looks like is a gargoyle. So it's also no coincidence that the princess in the fairy tale did not want to kiss the frog.

Nor is it a coincidence that many of the stories in this anthology are humorous. The title, *Ribbiting Tales*, invites comical stories. I owe the title to my ex-husband, punster Joel Springer. I'd like to acknowledge Martin H. Greenberg of Tekno-Books as the editor who first proposed an anthology of fantasy frog stories for children, and Michael Green of Philomel for his indefatigable efforts to make it the best collection it could be. I'd like to dedicate *Ribbiting Tales* to Michael, for in the words of a famous frog Muppet: "It's not easy being Green."

And thanks to David Lubar, author, for *that* pun. It's a sentiment echoed in several of the stories herein. Finally, I'd like to say that I hope you enjoy reading these stories as much as I enjoyed discovering them. *Ribbit!*

—Nancy Springer

Old Jim Croaker Jumps over the Moon

BY ROBERT J. HARRIS

. . .

ROUND ABOUT SUNSET, A BUNCH OF ELDERLY FROGS GATH-ered by the edge of the pond to pick off some of the lazier flies and tell tales of the old days, when frogs were really frogs and none of 'em would give a toad the time of day. As usual, the talk turned to Old Jim Croaker.

"I 'member the time Old Jim Croaker fought a water snake," one chortled. "He grabbed that thing in his yap and shook it around till it didn't know its head from its tail."

"That's nothing!" one of his friends croaked. "I know a story about Jim Croaker and the Talking Tree that's the thigh-slappinest yarn you ever heard."

At this point all of the old frogs started talking at once, each one insisting that he had the most amazing tale to tell.

Finally one of them raised his voice above all the others and boomed,

"If you want to hear a *real* Old Jim Croaker story, I've got one that'll put your flippers in a flap. Did you ever hear how Old Jim Croaker jumped over the Moon?"

This reduced the whole group to silence. They all looked blankly at one another, then croaked, "No, can't say as we ever did."

"Well, then, if you'll hush up for a spell, I'll tell you all about it. It happened like this.

IT WAS SPRINGTIME and Old Jim Croaker had a mind to do some courting. He had his sights set on a pretty little lady frog called Miss Pollywog Pearl. She was speckled bright green like pondweed, with a curly tongue that would make any upstanding he-frog go weak at the knees, and Old Jim wasn't the only one making extra-big goggle eyes at her.

One particular day, a whole crowd of young frogs was gathered around her, puffing up their neck sacks and bragging about how many flies they could catch in one lick. Old Jim Croaker sashayed over to the company and drummed his big flat feet on a lily pad to try and get Miss Pollywog Pearl's attention. Just then, however, she was listening to Buck Leaper sound off about how he once jumped right into the branches of the hickory tree down by the Rippling Creek.

Now, to any young frog with courting on his mind, bragging often seems a lot more important than doing. No sooner had Buck Leaper said his piece than Flip Flatfoot piped up, claiming he once jumped to the top of the pine tree by Frogwater Bridge. Then more and more of 'em up and spoke, each one telling how high he could leap. They let their mouths run away with them like a kingfisher taking off with a sprat until the whole business got pretty rowdy.

Old Jim Croaker could see he was going to have to top them all if he wanted Miss Pollywog Pearl to look favorable on him, so he puffed himself up real big and let out a bull-throated croak that drowned out all the rest of those boasters.

"I once jumped clear over the Moon!" he boomed, loud enough to send ripples over the water.

As you might expect, this shut everybody up pretty sharply and all eyes turned on him, especially Miss Pollywog Pearl's. She let her tongue hang out like she'd just spotted the juiciest fly that ever buzzed out of the reeds.

This wasn't lost on Buck Leaper, who hopped right in front of Old Jim Croaker and faced him chin to chin. "That's a plain lie!" he declared. "You couldn't jump any higher than your own fat head!"

Now this came as something of a shock to the whole crowd. Everybody knows that bragging is just bragging, and nobody expects to have to back it up. On the other hand, some of them did feel that Jim had brought it on himself by getting so downright preposterous.

Jim swelled himself up, doing his best to look cocky. "I done it," he insisted. "Lots of times."

"Then how come nobody ain't never seen you do it?" Buck Leaper challenged.

"I can only do it at night, you darned fool," Jim told him. "That's just common sense. That's why ain't nobody seen me do it."

Jim was still hoping that if he could only bluff hard enough, this whole thing might blow over like a summer thunder shower. But Buck Leaper had conceived a powerful longing for Miss Pollywog Pearl and he wasn't about to let go that easy.

"So what you're saying is, that if we was all to meet right here tonight, we could watch you jump over the Moon?" Buck was all spit and scorn.

"Yes, you could," Jim threw right back at him, "if I was of a mind to do it."

Buck belched a laugh, right in Jim's face, and quite a few of the other frogs joined in. It was not a pretty moment.

"It *would* be something to see," Miss Pollywog Pearl said sweetly.

Jim looked at her and when he saw how big her eyes bulged, and how her skin shone, his heart started pounding like a woodpecker drilling a tree.

"I'll do it for you, Miss Pearl," he said. The words kind of fell out of his gaping mouth of their own accord, along with every grain of sense he'd ever possessed.

"Then it's settled," Buck Leaper declared, real decisive. "We'll all get together here, tonight when the Moon's full."

"Sure," Old Jim Croaker agreed, hopping toward Miss Pollywog Pearl with his tongue dangling over his belly.

Miss Pollywog Pearl tilted her

head coyly. "See you tonight, Jim." Then she turned around and hopped off into the weeds.

Jim bumped to a stop and at last his brain started talking sense to the rest of his anatomy. He realized he was going to have to make good his bragging before Miss Pollywog Pearl would accept his advances.

That could be a problem. Even for Jim.

Now Jim was famous for his quick wits, and in about an hour he'd thought up a dozen different ways he could fake a jump to the Moon or lie his way out of the whole mess, but none of them was guaranteed to get him what he wanted. If Miss Pollywog Pearl thought he'd pulled a trick on her, she'd latch onto Buck Leaper quicker than a newt bags a dragonfly.

At a time like this there was only one thing to do, and that was to go talk to his uncle, Gatetrap Green.

Gatetrap Green had been pretty famous in his own heyday. It was said that he'd once ridden on the back of a specially dumb cat and used it to chase a gang of uppity toads back to the brush-wood they'd hopped from. These days he preferred to rest on his laurels and pursue more leisurely pastimes.

Gatetrap was lazing on his back by the side of the creek with his forelegs folded over his paunch when Jim found him. He looked like he was asleep, but as soon as Jim landed next to him his eyes snapped open.

"Howdy there, Jim," Gatetrap croaked, and closed his eyes up again.

"Gatetrap, I got me a problem," Jim announced.

Gatetrap opened one eye. "You're a smart boy. Think your way out of it."

"It ain't that simple this time," Jim said, and he explained the situation.

Gatetrap had done more than his fair share of courting in his youth and he gave a sympathetic smile.

"Jumping over the Moon, eh?" he mused. "It can be done, but it ain't easy. Looks to me like you got the flippers for it, though."

"But I ain't never jumped near that high before," Jim protested.

"That's because you only jumped once, then stopped."

Jim let out a puzzled croak.

"What do you do once you've jumped off the ground?" Gatetrap asked.

"Fall back down," Jim answered. "That's only natural."

"There's nothing you can teach me about Nature," Gatetrap told him. "The point is, instead of falling back down, you need to jump again. Bet you ain't never even tried it."

"Well, it ain't never crossed my mind," Jim admitted.

Gatetrap gave a knowing nod. "First you jump off the ground," he explained patiently, "then you got to jump off the air. That jump will take you higher, but only as high as the clouds."

"So what do I do then?" Jim asked.

"Well, next, before you start to fall again, you got to jump off the clouds. That'll take you real high—right up to the top of the sky. Then last of all you got to jump off the top of the sky. That last jump is the one that'll take you right past the Moon."

"It's that simple?" Jim asked, sounding a mite dubious.

"Oh, that part's real simple," Gatetrap told him. "It's the other part that's tricky."

"The other part?" Jim repeated.

"Yeah, getting back down."

"Oh," said Jim. He knew there had to be a catch.

"You see, once you done jumped that far, you kinda just keep on going, all the way out into the Inky Black."

Jim gulped. That didn't sound good.

"So here's what you have to do," Gatetrap said.

Jim listened to what his uncle had to tell him, then drummed his flippers nervously on the grass. "Will it work?" he asked.

"You'll be the first to find out," Gatetrap replied.

By the time the Moon had risen high in the sky that night, there was quite a crowd gathered around the edge of the pond. And you never heard such an uproar of croaking as there was when Jim hopped into their midst.

"So you decided to show your face," Buck Leaper said. There was scorn written all over him.

"Take a good look at it, Buck. See it grinning?" Jim answered.

He was grinning all right, but only on the outside. To tell the truth, he'd half hoped nobody would show up and that by morning the whole business would be forgotten. Instead, the crowd was even bigger than he'd feared.

Miss Pollywog Pearl was there in a place of honor on the biggest lily pad they could find for her. Jim acknowledged her with a modest bow of the head.

"Good luck, Jim," she sang out so sweetly it almost gave him courage.

Jim looked up at the Moon, all round and silver up above, and tried to convince himself that it didn't look so very far away.

"Well, we're waiting." Buck Leaper sneered.

"It would be easier for me and safer for you if you'd oblige me by hopping back a space, Buck," Jim said haughtily.

Buck Leaper jumped back and for the first time there was some doubt in his eyes. He looked from Jim to the Moon and back again, then slowly shook his head.

There was a tingle of anticipation in the air and the whole crowd fell quiet while Jim made a big show of limbering up his legs and bracing himself for the jump. It occurred to him that he could still drag himself out of this mess—not without a lot of shame, it must be admitted—by pretending to sprain his leg just as he went into his crouch. Then he looked over at Miss Pollywog Pearl, and *those kind of thoughts* came back to him so strongly that he felt intoxicated.

He sank into a crouch and tensed his leg muscles. Staring up at the Moon, he took three deep breaths and . . .

LEAPT!

It was the highest jump Jim Croaker had ever made in his life, but the Moon didn't look even a whit closer. As soon as he'd reached the peak of his jump, he flexed his legs and jumped again, launching himself higher into the night.

Jumping off the air carried him higher and faster, and he could feel the breeze whistling over his skin. He caught his breath as he sensed the highest point of this leap approach. At that moment he pumped his legs hard and jumped again, right off the clouds and up into the yawning dark with the Moon blazing in its center.

Now the Moon had gotten bigger and it was gawking at him in mute surprise. Jim gasped and didn't even think of looking back to see the stunned expressions on the other frogs' faces. If Gatetrap was right, there was only one leap left to go, and that would carry him past the Moon. He could feel himself slowing down and he knew that he could either fall short of the Moon and tumble back to Earth or make that last push and risk being lost forever in the Inky Black.

Maybe by now his head was so full of speed and excitement that there wasn't any other decision he could make, but as soon as he felt himself teeter on the edge of a fall, Jim pumped his legs for all they were worth and flung himself straight at the Moon.

He came bouncing off the top of the sky, so fast and free that for a moment all fear was forgotten in the heady rush. He'd done it! He'd put his legs where his mouth was!

The Moon winked at Jim as he flew past, and all at once he realized to his horror that if he didn't do something real fast, he was going to keep on going right out into the Inky Black with only the flickering stars

to keep him company. He remembered, in the midst of the heady rush of jumping, what Uncle Gatetrap had told him. He had only one chance to get back to Miss Pollywog Pearl, and quick as a flash, he took it.

He twisted his head around and whipped out his tongue. It lashed out across the cold night and smacked the Moon square in the right eye. With the end of his tongue fixed onto the Moon's cold face, Jim held on for all he was worth as he shot past the edge of the silver disk.

"Hey!" the Moon yelled. "What's going on here?"

Jim was in no position to answer. He was whirling around the back of the Moon so fast it made him dizzy. His tongue was stretched so tight he could hear it twang.

Goggle-eyed, he saw the world swing back into sight and it was so far below it made his belly lurch. In the same second, he let go of the Moon and went shooting back homeward like a seed that's been spat at the ground. The Moon's eye was smarting and Jim could hear it cussing him out as he plummeted toward Earth.

A crowd of incredulous faces gaped up at him as he came whooshing out of the night to splash down right in the middle of the pond. He hit the surface so hard he sent up a waterspout that knocked a passing buzzard clean out of the sky.

A couple of the frogs jumped in after Jim and dragged him up onto the bank. He was kind of bashed up, but he had nothing broken that wouldn't mend. He lay there gasping, his jaw hanging loose, his brain still spinning from the trip. Miss Pollywog Pearl came and cooed over him in admiration, but Jim was too far gone to notice. He spent the next three weeks wrapped in wet grass with his friends bringing him flies and pondweed at regular intervals to assist his convalescence.

By the time he'd recovered his senses and went looking for Miss Pollywog Pearl, she'd already run off with Buck Leaper, so there was no joy at all that spring for Old Jim Croaker.

A tall tale, you say? Well, you just take a good look at the Moon tonight, and you'll see its right eye's still swollen where Jim smacked it with his tongue. And I can tell you one thing for sure. Old Jim better not try jumping up there again or the Moon is liable to smack *him* in the face this time, and Jim could do with not looking any worse than he does now if he ever wants to go courting again.

Delia Broom and the Frog-People of Quicksand Pond

BY JANET TAYLOR LISLE

• • •

From *The Swampton Weekly Gazette*, Thursday, October 1:

IT'S NO FAIRY TALE:
PHOTOS REVEAL HALF-HUMAN FROGS

Amazing photographs taken last week of a previously unknown species of frog living in South County's Quicksand Pond have sent ripples through nearby communities.

The frogs appear to have developed some human physical characteristics, including necks and arms. Whether the mutant strain has been here all along, hidden within the primordial bog that surrounds this pond, or evolved recently is among the questions already under investigation by a team of prominent scientists and biologists.

The photos were taken when a twelve-year-old camera buff, looking for her lost cat, stumbled on . . ."

SHE HAD NOT STUMBLED, of course. Newspapers always get things wrong. Delia Broom was not a stumbler. She walked precisely, attentively, with a sharp eye for detail—exactly the way she took her photographs.

And she had certainly not been looking for her cat. That was ridiculous. You don't go around looking for a cat that has been lost for almost a year. You might think about him, yes. You might go around remembering his thick, velvety fur and enormous paws. Six-toed paws, Roderick had. He left tracks the size of a wolf's. But he was beautiful, too: the way he moved—like a dancer; the honey gold color of his eyes.

Sometimes in the late afternoon, Delia Broom goes out in the field behind her house where this cat was last seen. She gazes across the darkening surface of the pond and thinks of calling: "Roderick!" As she used to. "Roderick! Come for supper!"

But she doesn't call. Not anymore. Instead, she walks slowly down to the edge of the pond, sits on the bank and *click*, takes a picture of the late afternoon sun shining on the water. (Not a bad shot.)

The bank may still be damp from a rainstorm last night but so what? Dampness, mud, they aren't things Delia Broom notices. She is not one of those photographers who are afraid of getting their feet wet. Though the water is getting colder now. Autumn is well underway in this salt pond near the sea. The reeds are beginning to turn from green to honey gold, the same honey gold shade as . . .

Click. Nice colors there. Hope that one comes out.

Three seagulls fly over (*click, click*) giving out the plaintive mews that seagulls make when they are speaking among themselves of seagull matters. Of migrating shoals of fish, or beds of juicy mussels nestled along the shore. Of food in many forms—what most wild creatures are thinking about at this time of year, not only birds but muskrats, mink, rabbits, deer . . . coyotes. Everyone is looking for a good meal. The chilly nights give warning: last call to fatten up before winter's frigid fast. Even cats get this message.

Roderick liked to hunt in the field. In the fall, he'd be out in it all day. He was an expert mouser and enjoyed tracking moles, rabbits, chipmunks. He'd always come home for supper, though, and spend the night indoors. There was a good reason.

Some nights, in the cold, black hours before dawn, Delia Broom would wake to hear a high, yelping wail outside her window. Coyotes. Their howls made the hair rise on the back of her neck. They kept a den somewhere west of the pond and had the run of the area because they were protected by law. Newly arrived, an endangered species from the north, they could not be hunted.

Everyone knew the Quicksand Pond coyotes liked to hunt at night. Roderick knew. He'd seen them: gaunt, yellow gray, wolfish-looking animals, always hungry but especially hungry in the fall. So hungry they'd come out before dark sometimes, while the sun was still setting and shadows striped the land. They'd pad out of the woods, lope silently toward the pond, spring suddenly into a field before a cat had gone indoors.

Then the cat would have to run for its life.

He'd have to sprint and leap and zig and zag and use every trick he knew to get home before ... before ...

Let us not say before what.

Late one afternoon, Delia Broom is sitting on the wet pond bank as usual, her camera around her neck. (She never travels without it.) She is looking out across the darkening water, remembering her lost cat, Roderick, trying not to think of what might have happened, when there's a rustle in the grass to the right.

She jumps a little, twists around and sees something move. She gets up warily and goes over to investigate. That's when she sees them for the first time: a cluster of little creatures surging busily here and there, gathering red berries from a bush at the pond's edge.

She thinks they're some large type of hummingbird at first. They are green all over, flying off the ground, or bouncing maybe because their wings look folded. Then she looks closer and realizes that they don't have wings. Those are arms. And they have half-bent, froglike legs. And brownish green hands and feet that are webbed at the end, no fingers or toes.

Maybe she gives a little gasp as she crouches down and focuses the camera for a shot (*click, click*). Or maybe her shadow falls over them because just then, quicker than lightning, they look up and see her and are gone. Like that. One moment Delia Broom sees the flash of their big, frightened eyes looking up out of their flat froggish faces (*click*), the next moment—empty space.

She lowers the camera, glances about, but there is no sign of anything except, down by the bank, some water ripples fanning out slowly into the pond, growing wider and wider.

Naturally, in the next minute, Delia Broom is wondering if she saw what she thinks she saw. She can't wait to get home and develop the photos. There's nothing like a photograph for showing the truth. It's time to go home, anyway. Past time. The sun has dropped behind the horizon. The evening is turning rapidly dark and cold.

Delia starts to walk home fast, a little nervous about running into a coyote cruising the field. Or worse, a pack of coyotes. It's unfair, she thinks, that these coyotes get to go around carefree and unhunted, preying on cats or whomever they want. They should have their predators, too. They should have to feel afraid, the way they make others feel, including, at this very moment, Delia Broom, who now begins to race at top speed across the field toward home.

From *The Swampton Weekly Gazette*, Thursday, October 8:

EXPERTS WARY OF LEAPING TO CONCLUSIONS ON RARE FROGS

A team of top biologists confirmed yesterday that an unknown species of frog photographed recently in South County township's Quicksand Pond area does seem to display characteristics that strongly resemble the human body.

The frogs, which were photographed by a young photographer at dusk on September 28, show well-developed necks, shoulders, and arms. Heads, however, retain frog shape and features, including jowls and wide-spaced, bulging eyes.

The creatures, which are each about the size of a large hummingbird, appear in the photos to be foraging for food on the pond bank, according to Dr. Edward Biltmore of Lovelace University's Biological Labs, Inc., a nonprofit research group.

Dr. Biltmore said scientists remain skeptical but are intrigued by the photos, which were tested for authenticity and found reliable.

"We have set up fine-mesh fencing and positioned watch teams

around the pond in hopes of further glimpses of these rare creatures, and perhaps even of capturing one," Dr. Biltmore said.

Meanwhile, Delia Broom, the twelve-year-old photographer who snapped the photos, warned researchers about coyotes in the area that may threaten the frogs. Interviewed by reporters at her home yesterday, she told of witnessing an attack on one frog colony by coyotes who encircled their victims and then . . .

"IT WAS HORRIBLE TO WATCH."

(This is the story Delia tells the reporters.)

"I was sitting on the pond bank when it happened. What time? Oh, about 4 P.M. I guess. After school, anyway, like the first time. I'd been keeping my eyes open all week for any other strange appearances. So I noticed when the sound started up.

"It was a humming noise, sort of, from a place farther down the pond's edge. I tiptoed over, ready to photograph more evidence. I guess I knew already what would be there. And that's exactly what it was: the frog-people again.

"They were crouched around in a ring having some kind of ceremony. The noises came from their throats, like purring. I was just raising my camera to take a picture when these high, wailing barks broke out and four huge coyotes sprang through the tall grass. They pounced on the frogs. I was so shocked! I stood there with my mouth open. I meant to scream but never did. I never took the photo either. That's why there isn't one.

"What happened then? Well, just what you'd expect. The coyotes began to eat up the little frog-people with terrible chomps and gulps. They swallowed most of them in a matter of seconds. A few frogs escaped into the pond. I saw bubbles rise near the bank. The coyotes barked angrily after them and scratched up mud. Coyotes don't like anything to get away.

"That's why I decided to warn Dr. Biltmore and the scientists who are investigating the frogs," Delia Broom tells the reporters, who are sitting around her living room taking notes as she speaks. "Rare and beautiful creatures are in danger. Some have already been lost. Not only frogs, but cats."

Cats? The reporters chuckle. Cats are hardly in the same category as a rare species of frog, are they?

"Oh, yes they are!" Delia Broom finds herself bellowing. "Cats are very important animals!"

When the reporters chuckle again, Delia ends the interview by marching furiously out of the room.

From *The Swampton Weekly Gazette*, Thursday, October 15:

SCIENTISTS ACT TO PROTECT ONE ENDANGERED SPECIES FROM ANOTHER

A group of biological scientists led by Dr. Edward Biltmore today petitioned the Federal Fish and Wildlife Service for permission to "hunt out and destroy" a pack of Eastern Mountain coyotes that has taken up residence west of South County's Quicksand Pond.

The action was taken after the animals, which are on the endangered species list themselves, attacked an even rarer and more endangered species of frog that is believed to be living around the pond area.

The frogs appear in recent photos to display some characteristics of the human torso, a surprising but not impossible evolutionary phenomenon, according to Dr. Biltmore, who is leading the research group.

"Frogs' internal organs and circulatory systems have many similarities to those of human beings," he said. "This is why frogs are often dissected in schools. The frog interior provides students with an excellent model of how the human body functions. It does not seem improbable, therefore, that some frogs may finally be evolving external human characteristics as well. We are excited by recent photos showing . . ."

IT'S AMAZING HOW MUCH attention a person can get from a few little stories in the newspaper!

One minute Delia Broom is a shy, quiet loner who spends half her time outside photographing animals and nature, and the other half in a darkroom developing her film.

The next minute she is being interviewed by radio and television reporters, telling the rather ordinary story of her life. She was born. She learned to talk. Her dad, Walker Broom, was the famous wildlife photographer who disappeared two years ago on assignment in Africa. He taught her everything she knows about photography, darkrooms, etc. Sure, she misses him, what a dumb question. He might still come home someday. Who knows? He might.

After getting through with her life, she answers more questions about her two meetings with the extraordinary frog-people. No, she hasn't seen them again, not since the coyote attack. Isn't twice enough?

Delia is getting so much better at interviews! She doesn't lose control of her temper now, and agrees to allow more reporters to interview her (though her mom is beginning to get kind of worried about all this) because she wants to make her point about coyotes more forcefully.

These animals are a clear and continuing threat to much-loved species of all kinds! They wreak havoc and leave shattered lives in their wake. No, Delia isn't out to get them, she just . . . thinks biological diversity is important. Endangered species must be protected!

When one rather sharp-nosed reporter asks if it isn't true that coyotes killed a cat belonging to her, Delia Broom, last year, Delia shrugs.

"This has nothing to do with cats," she replies in a chilly voice.

Meanwhile, the result of Dr. Biltmore's petition to the Federal Fish and Wildlife Service appears in the field below the Broom house one afternoon toward the middle of October. It is a small squad of men with guns. They are wearing bright orange hunting vests and caps. Delia walks down with her camera to see what's going on. One of the hunters comes forward to meet her. He asks, "Can you show us where the coyotes attacked the endangered frogs?"

"Yes, of course. Right over here. Near the pond's bank there's a little clearing. Here it is."

"And you were standing where?"

"Oh, back over there. I tried to take a photo, but it happened too fast."

"But you saw the coyotes. How many were there?"

"Four, I think. They came so quickly."

"The reason I ask," the orange-vested lead hunter says, "is it's a little strange. This type of coyote doesn't normally hunt in packs."

"Oh. Well, there were at least three, I think. Or maybe two. Do they ever hunt in pairs?"

"They do. It's more likely."

"Well, now that I think about it, two does seem more the right number."

"There's one other thing," the orange-vested hunter goes on. "Coyotes are usually not much interested in frogs. Too small, you know? They like larger, juicier game—rabbits, groundhogs. Cats, for that matter."

"Well, I know." Delia gazes briefly across the pond, then brings her eyes back. "But that's the thing about these frogs."

"What's the thing?"

"They have more to them . . . than ordinary frogs, I mean. They're kind of like small human beings. Maybe they smell different than frogs. And taste better."

"Hmmm," says the lead hunter, giving Delia a quick look. "We've found the tracks of only one animal so far. He's a big fellow. Leaves enormous tracks. Walks with a limp. Probably been around here awhile."

"Enormous tracks?" Delia echoes.

"Yup. Big for coyote tracks. About the size of a wolf's."

When this conversation is ended, Delia walks thoughtfully around the pond to where the mesh fencing of the scientists is set up. After a week of staking out the pond, no one has reported seeing any of the frogs.

"I hope they didn't all get eaten by the coyotes," Dr. Biltmore worries to Delia when she finds him.

She sits down next to him on the bank and takes a few photos (click, click) of him peering through his binoculars. He looks a little like a grasshopper—flat eyes, long nose, silver-rimmed spectacles whose wire stems loop up over his large ears like antennae. Delia leans back and stares at him. For a minute, it looks as if she's about to ask him something. Then she shakes her head, as if dismissing some worry, and glances away. Car horns blow loudly in the distance. There is a rumble of wheels.

"Now who can that be?" Dr. Biltmore inquires.

From *The Swampton Weekly Gazette*, Thursday, October 22:

QUICKSAND POND FROG-PEOPLE DRAW SURGING CROWDS

Reports of frogs that resemble small human beings and live in South County's Quicksand Pond attracted crowds of sightseers to the area this past weekend.

Local homeowners complained of noisy traffic jams that blocked their driveways and of trampled hedges and gardens as hoards of people converged on the pond with binoculars and cameras.

Township police were called in to keep control. Fire department volunteers arrived with rescue vehicles when one woman fainted at the pond's edge.

"I saw one! I saw one!" screamed Marianne Childs, of Rocky Point, moments before she fainted and collapsed on the bank. She was taken immediately to South County Hospital, where she was treated for minor bruises and released.

Childs said later she had seen one of the frog-people, but others standing near her could not confirm her sighting.

Meanwhile, scientists from Lovelace University's Biologic Labs, Inc., said isolated sightings of the frog-people, as the mysterious frogs are being called, are being reported in growing numbers.

The creatures, which appear to have human torsos and make a vibrating noise that sounds like a cat's purr, have been seen on the west, east, and northern edges of the pond, and paddling south across the water on small pieces of wood resembling dugout canoes.

Dr. Edward Biltmore, of the university, said he and his staff are attempting to investigate all sightings.

"We have no certain evidence of the existence of these frog-people, but are remaining hopeful," Dr. Biltmore said, adding that he has asked police to seal off the area so that important scientific evidence is not trampled.

In related activity, a group of Fish and Wildlife Service sharp-shooters located an abandoned coyote den in a shrub thicket west of the pond. The sharpshooters were called in after one frog colony was reportedly devoured by a pack of coyotes.

"The coyotes that occupied this den moved on some time ago," said John Rinaldi, chief of Wildlife Management in the South County area. "We are currently tracking another large animal who leaves six-toed paw prints. The animal walks with a distinctive limp. Its tracks, which resemble a wolf's, center around a deserted cabin in a heavily forested section of South County Reservation about three miles south of Quicksand Pond. Hikers are urged not to use trails in this area until . . ."

SIX-TOED PAW PRINTS!

It is Thursday afternoon. Delia, just home from school, is reading this article when, coming upon the words *six-toed paw prints*, she drops the newspaper and lets out a terrified shriek.

A second later, she is racing into her darkroom. She grabs the frog photos she took three weeks ago, hurtles out the door, and sprints down into the field to find Dr. Edward Biltmore—before it's too late!

There he is, thank heavens, hopping with his grasshopperish leap over the fine-mesh fencing, just disappearing around a curve in the pond.

"Wait!" Delia screams. "I need to tell you something! Dr. Biltmore, please wait!"

He turns, wearing a friendly smile, and when Delia comes panting up she tells him, straight out with no introduction, "I lied!"

"What?" His smile fades.

"I made up the frog-people. There aren't any."

"But, but . . ." Total scientific confusion. "What about the photos? They tested out. They're authentic," he sputters. "Our specialists said so."

"They aren't authentic! I made them look that way," Delia yells. "I took photos of some plastic toy aliens I had when I was a kid. I fixed the photos up! I swear it! I know how to do it."

"Why, you little snake!" Dr. Biltmore looks furious.

"So you can call off the sharpshooters. That was a lie, too," Delia says.

"What was?"

"The coyotes never attacked the frogs. I made that up to get in the newspaper."

"This is outrageous! Wait until I tell your mother! What kind of mother do you have, anyway, to let you get away with something like this?"

Delia hangs her head. "A really great one, actually. It isn't her fault. Since my dad got lost, she has to work all the time to get us through. She misses him a lot and doesn't always notice what I do."

Dr. Biltmore's face softens. He pats her arm and decides that Delia Broom is a confused child still suffering from her father's tragic disappearance in the wilds of Africa, and he lets her off the hook. He is a kind man with a big heart who just happens to look like a grasshopper. He can't help it.

"I knew your dad," he says suddenly.

"You did?"

"A little. Long ago. He's a fine photographer. Any chance he'll be found?"

"I don't know," Delia says. "It's been a long time." She lets out a deep sigh.

Within hours of Delia's amazing confession, Dr. Biltmore packs up his scientific gear, rallies his scientists, and tells everyone to go home. He also calls the Federal Fish and Wildlife Service and orders them to stop sending hunters to destroy the coyotes at Quicksand Pond.

"It was all a misunderstanding," he tells the feds, the university, the scientists, and, in an exclusive interview, *The Swampton Weekly Gazette*. "Though if you ask me, I'd still swear those photos are authentic," he adds quietly. "The negatives tested out. They're as real as they come."

No one is in a mood to ask him anything, however. Many people are angry. They feel tricked and used. Others think it's funny. They say they never believed in any frog-people anyway, so what's the difference?

And with that, the story of how Delia Broom, expert camera buff, invented the frog-people of Quicksand Pond to take revenge on the terrible coyotes who killed Roderick, her golden-eyed, enormous-pawed, six-toed cat, comes to an end.

Except for one thing.

Toward evening on the same day she confessed to Dr. Biltmore, Delia takes a walk around the bank of Quicksand Pond, heading south toward the South County Reservation. She walks uphill, then downhill, following an old hiking trail into a densely wooded area. In all she goes some three miles.

The deserted cabin is exactly where the Fish and Wildlife Service hunters described it as being, beside a little stream in the woods.

It's very quiet here. Very lost and lonely. The lowering sun shines with a honey gold brilliance through the trees surrounding the cabin. Delia sits down a little way away and *click*, takes a picture. (That was nice.)

Click. Click. Evening approaches slowly and, except for a few chirping birds, silently.

After a while, Delia catches sight of movement in some underbrush near the cabin. She holds her breath, and a moment later a large animal comes out of the bushes carrying in its mouth a dead mole.

The animal is limping. Something has mangled his right front leg and made him lame. Such accidents happen in the wild. You often can't know with certainty whether a simple fall, an attack by a ferocious animal, a hunter's trap, a speeding car, or any of a dozen other mishaps have caused injury to the stricken animal, have perhaps confused his brain so that he forgets where he is, and becomes lost, and is separated from his home.

"Roderick!"

Delia calls him in the softest voice, not wanting to scare him after all this time.

"Roderick, come for supper!"

The big cat with the thick, velvety mane turns his head and looks at her. He drops the mole and stares. Then, without taking his eyes off her for a moment, he begins to run toward her on his enormous paws. Like a dancer he moves, except for his limp—like a dancer who suddenly remembers everything, everyone, and *click!, click!* she takes his picture that way, running for her arms, coming home.

It Came from Outer Little Pond

BY BRIAN JACQUES

• • •

IT STARTED EARLY ONE SPRING MORNING WITH A THUD-ding around one side of Little Pond. This was followed by a splash, and then the thudding died away. Beneath the pond surface, amid weeds, pebbles, and mud, King Obluk and his frogs lay groggy after sleeping all winter. His Majesty, Obluk, raised one eyelid, still sleepy and in a totally foul frogmood.

"Lubwok, go and see who is disturbing our royal snooze!"

Reluctantly Lubwok dislodged himself from the ooze and swam sluggishly off to do his king's bidding. A moment later he shot back like a scorched wasp, fully awake. Burrowing into the mud he cowered there, trembling. King Obluk kicked him—he enjoyed kicking his subjects— so he kicked Lubwok once more and felt all the better for it.

"Unmud yourself and report to me, oaf!"

Lubwok poked his head out of the mud and jabbered like a demented water beetle. "Up there! Up there, Majesty! A big flue brog with sped rots! I saw it myself, a flog, all brue with spet rods!"

Queen Grobug opened both her eyes and blinked regally. "What is that nitbrain yammering on about, my dear!"

King Obluk sighed, raised his bulk up, and sat on Lubwok's head. "Huh, who knows, my sweet. I'll just smother him awhile until he regains his senses, the louse-witted buffoon!"

Soon Lubwok began flopping his webs for mercy. King Obluk raised his bulk, but only slightly.

"Well, Lubwok, feeling recovered enough to talk slowly and sensibly to your king now, eh?"

As clearly as he could, under the circumstances, Lubwok spoke. "Sire, there's a big blue frog with red spots swimming around in your pond. I saw it with my own eyes, Majesty!"

At that, the queen came over and sat on Lubwok's head with her husband, to discuss the situation. "He's been eating water beetles again, Obby, driven himself dotty by the sound of it. What d'you think?"

King Obluk whispered confidentially to her. "Please don't call me Obby in front of our subjects, dear."

He raised his voice then, for the benefit of all his frog subjects. "I need some frog to go and see what really is up there!"

The frogs all buried themselves deeper in the mud, pretending they had not heard a word King Obluk had uttered. Except for one, a very tiny fellow named Oikk, who had been a late-developing tadpole from last season. "I'm not afraid, Sire. Let *me* go!"

Still sitting on Lubwok's head, the king and queen shook with laughter, both royal bottoms causing poor Lubwok great discomfort. The king blew a scornful bubble at Oikk. "Go away and don't bother me, tiddle-tail. Droople! Plongg! Get your idle webs up there and scout around. Report back to me, quick as you can. That's a command!"

The two nosy sisters, Droople and Plongg, were quite eager to see what had frightened Lubwok, and swam off swiftly. Queen Grobug nodded approvingly.

"They'll get the job done, Obby. Oh, look, Lubwok's gone a funny color and he's blowing little bubbles."

King Obluk tried counting the bubbles but lost interest. "Probably all those water beetles he's been munching. I've warned him about that often, and I've also cautioned you, madam, about calling me Obby—it's not very dignified!"

Droople and Plongg broke the surface, just in time to jointly receive a smack in the eye. They croaked out in pain and retreated to the reeds to watch the thing, horrified at what they saw. It was a huge blue frog, with red polka-dot spots all over its body, swimming speedily around the pond. Droople murmured in fear. "I've never seen anything like that in all frogdom!"

Plongg dragged her sister beneath the surface. "Nor have I. We'd better report back quick!"

When the sisters returned, King Obluk shook his head in disbelief. He waggled a web at the two frogs, each clutching her injured eye as their ruler worked himself into a fine old frenzy. "I'm going to put a stop to all this water beetle eating, just you see if I don't. You've heard the expression 'Mad as fried frogs in a bucket'? Well, that's the way you lot will end up if you continue pigging down water beetles. What's wrong with good old mud worms? I was reared on them. You don't see me going around gabbling about big blue frogs with red spots, do you? No! Out of the way there, I'm going to see this thing for myself, and if there is a big blue frog covered in red spots trespassing in my pond, I'll give it a piece of my mind!"

Lubwok sighed with relief as the king hopped off his head and swam upward in high dudgeon, with the queen calling anxiously after him. "Do be careful, Obby! Remember your frog pressure and try to keep your temper under control; you're not a tadpole anymore!"

Lubwok rubbed the side of his head where the king had sat. "Huh, you can say that again, marm!"

Queen Grobug settled herself more firmly on his head. "What was that you said, Lubwok?"

"Oh, Queen, I said I hope His Majesty doesn't come to any harm...."

King Obluk was about to surface when he looked up and saw the big, blue, red-spotted frog swim by overhead, so he waited until it had passed, then poked his head up above water level. Summing up every ounce of courage, King Obluk puffed out his cheeks and throat, managing to look the fearsome picture of regal indignation. He bellowed after the speedily swimming creature. "You there! Red spotty bluefrog! What d'you think you're up to, eh? Swimming around my pond without as much as a 'beg y'pardon' or 'by your leave.' Stop! Stop I say!"

The big frog never stopped. Instead, it made a strange noise and turned, heading straight for the king. Obluk trod water, his chin stuck defiantly out, his fighting spirit roused. "Do you know who I am, sir? I'm King Obluk, ruler of all frogs within Little Pond! Tsar of Tadpoles!

Master of the Mud! Defender of the Reeds! Scourge of Water-Beetle Eaters! Stop I say and begone from my realm!"

But the big frog kept coming at an alarming speed. The king thrust his chin out farther, seething with wrath. "Have a care, or I'll kick you several times and sit on your red-spotted blue head, just see if I don't! You'll rue the da . . ."

Thuddo! The big frog butted King Obluk right under his chin and swam onward without a single word.

When the king regained consciousness, his queen and several other capable frog matrons were applying a water lily and duckweed compress to the nasty swelling under his chin, as this is a sovereign remedy for a sore chin, as any frog knows, and reckoned to be far more efficacious when applied to the chin of a sovereign. Pushing them irately from him, King Obluk roared out an order, which was quite difficult to comprehend, seeing as he had bitten his tongue when the big frog butted his chin. "Thend for Yigbul! Where'th Yigbul, I mutht know!"

Yigbul, royal champion and the queen's favorite assassin, lumbered through the mud, made a frogsleg and bowed. "Your word is my command, Sire!"

"Athathinate that blue thpotty frog inthtantly!"

The hulking Yigbul stood puzzled, until the queen translated. "Go and slay that frog who attacked poor Obby!"

As Yigbul went to do the deed, the king winced. "I thaid not to call me Obby in front of the frogth, dear!"

Little Oikk hopped about anxiously. "Please let me go and help him, Majesties, oh, please!"

King Obluk glowered at him. "Oh, thyuttup, you inthignificant petht!"

Yigbul returned moments later with a lump that looked like a big tadpole growing out of his skull. King Obluk clutched his head despairingly. "Well, tell uth what took plathe, Yigbul."

"I came up behind

him, Sire, but he kicked out with both back legs and near broke my head. I'm sorry, Your Majesty."

King Obluk ranted, completely forgetting his injury and his frog pressure. He was at the end of his royal tether. "Thorry? You're thorry? Oh, woe ith me, ith there no frog in thith pond to rid me of this red-thpotted pethtilenth? I will give him anything he de-thireth!"

Little Oikk shot off like an arrow. "Leave it to me, Sire!"

The king watched him go, sadly. "He'll be thlain."

They waited in silence as the moments dragged by, every frog expecting to see Oikk's tiny carcass drifting lifelessly downward at any instant. Poor Oikk, he was no bigger than a water beetle.

Then thumping noises sounded from above, followed by several loud splashes. King Obluk and his queen huddled together, making sure all the other frogs were on top of them for protection. Lubwok sat on the king's head, smiling maliciously. He even managed to kick the queen (purely by accident, of course).

Then there was silence from above. Eerie, deathly silence. Little Oikk swam briskly down and gave both majesties his best bow before announcing, "Fear not, I slew the monster and slung him out of the pond!"

Little Oikk explained the long, desperate fight with the big, blue, red-spotted frog. King Obluk and Queen Grobug, and every other frog in Little Pond, were visibly impressed. They gasped when he told how he had ridden on the monster's back around the pond three times, throttling it furiously until it was dead. Then there was the web-thrilling account of how Oikk had flung the monster bodily from the pond, where it was snatched up by some beast and eaten.

King Obluk heaped the tiny warrior with honors. "From forthwith you thyall be known ath Oikk, King'th Athathin. All frogth mutht bow to you, and you thyall wear a green jacket with golden frogging!"

The frog subjects all cheered and croaked themselves hoarse. Queen Grobug even let Oikk sit on her head, as he was very light and looked quite decorative in his new jacket. She smiled as she reached up and patted his webs. "My, my, don't we look absolutely charming, Oikky?"

The little frog sniffed, drawing himself up to the full height of a royal assassin. "Yes, Majesty, but please don't call me Oikky in front of these other common frogs!"

MR. BIGELOW WATCHED his two children, Georgie and Katy, dash into the living room. "Whoa there, you two, wipe your feet after coming through the woods and over the field. Well, did you find it?"

Georgie proudly held up the big battery-powered toy his father had bought him. It was all the rage for any kid who had seen the movie *Frognophobia* to own one. He touched the switch underneath it. Immediately the frog's limbs started working, swimming frantically in midair.

"I must've dropped it. Guess where it fell, Dad—right into Little Pond. That's where I found it."

Dad chuckled. "Was it swimming around enjoying itself?"

Katy giggled. "Oh, don't be so silly, Daddy, it was just floating around. We had to splash about with a stick and rescue it. The frog wasn't switched on!"

Her father winked and smiled. "Maybe it switched on when it fell out of Georgie's pocket, so it had a nice little swim around the pond."

Georgie liked his dad being silly. He went along with him. "That's right, Dad, and just before we came along, a little frog switched it off to save the batteries."

Katy shook her head. "Now you're both being silly!"

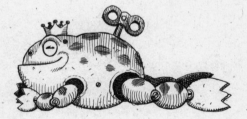

Green Plague

BY JANE YOLEN

• • •

IT WAS ONLY A SMALL VILLAGE HIGH UP IN THE MOUN-
tains, but the tourists loved it. The water was clean, the air fresh, and
the native population wore quaint costumes, not unlike the ones their
great-great-grandparents had worn, only made more comfortable with
zippers and Velcro fastenings.

The village's fortunes were based on the legend of a piper and a
plague of rats some five centuries earlier, and they had carefully culti-
vated it for the tourist trade.

Not that anyone believed the legend. As the mayor said, "A lie, but
our own."

And a very profitable lie it was. There were dioramas of the alleged
incident in the town hall. Schoolchildren, in their adorable costumes,
sang songs about the rats in the amphitheater for visitors, in German,
Spanish, Italian, French, English, and Japanese. Trips to the town's
cheese factories were the highlight of every tour, with twiddly oompa-
pa music piped in to the factory elevators. In fact, all of the brochures
about holidays in the little town were decorated with pictures of rats,
though they bore little resemblance to the rodents of old, but were as

cuddly as the plush toy mice that were sold in the village gift shop, along with plastic piccolos that could flute half an octave at best.

Very profitable indeed.

STILL THE TOWNSFOLK were more than a little surprised when they awoke one morning, less than a month till high season, to another kind of plague.

"Frogs!" thundered the village mayor to the hastily convened council. His fleshy jowls trembled with the word. He held one of the offending green invaders by a leg and waved it above his head.

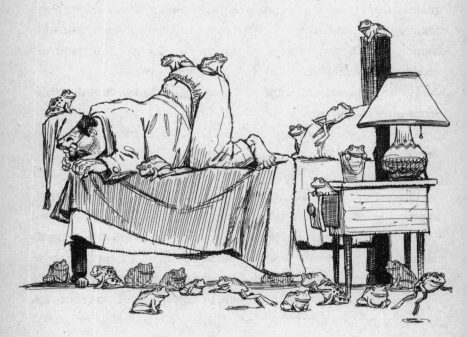

"They're everywhere," complained a thin-faced man who was the mayor's chief rival. He shuddered with distaste.

"In the bathtub," said one councilor.

"And the buttery," said another.

"Under the beds," said a third.

"And doing the breaststroke in the toilet bowl," thundered the mayor. He was popular for saying things plainly and because of it had been elected seven years in a row, a village record. "These frogs will ruin business. And we have just been named Attraction of the Year by the National Board of Tourism." They all knew that this was an important citation. It meant that booklets about the village would be in every guide and information shop in the country free of charge. It meant they could expect an increase in visitors of almost 300 percent in the upcoming year. "We must do something to rid ourselves of this green invasion," the mayor concluded.

The council wrestled for about an hour with the problem while green peepers, leopard frogs, and bullfrogs hopped about their feet.

At last the mayor thundered, "This is a plague of biblical proportions!"

"In proportion to what?" asked the thin man.

That started them on one of their epic arguments. No one expected to get out of council chambers until noon.

But just then a very large and hairy frog climbed onto the council table. Its eyes bulged in a horrible manner, as if any minute they were going to fall right out of its head.

"*Trichobatrachus robustus*," the thin man said, shuddering again as he did so, "from West Africa. I, at least, have been doing my homework."

The big frog stared right at the mayor, who, in a sudden panic, hastily adjourned the meeting until the early afternoon.

Gratefully, the councilors all fled the room, leaving the frogs in charge.

IN THE CENTER OF THE VILLAGE, the full extent of the green plague could now be seen. What had been a trickle of family Ranidae at breakfast had, by lunch, become a tidal wave.

Put simply: There were frogs everywhere.

Some were small green blobs and some were enormous ten-inch-round boulders. They seemed to stretch from the foot of Grossmutter to the foot of Harlingberg, the two mountains that made up the sides of the village's valley.

The children were the only ones who were enjoying the spectacle. They had abandoned their own games of tag and hide-and-seek to start frog racing and frog-jumping contests with the more agreeable frogs.

But as frogs continued to flood into the town, even the children lost interest. A frog or two or seven in the street is one thing. But a frog floating languidly in your milk glass or curled up on your pillow or draped across your toothbrush is another.

BY EVENING THE FROGS outnumbered the citizens by a thousandfold. And still the green plague continued.

"We need a piper!" the mayor whispered. A day of thundering had reduced his vocal chords to single notes. The councilors had to strain to hear him in a room now crowded with frogs who were peeping and thrumming and harrumphing with spring pleasure.

At that point, everyone on the council—and the mayor himself—trooped down to the village gift shop and tried tootling on the plastic piccolos. They hoped, one and all, that the legend might actually have some base in reality. But tootle as they might, it was soon quite clear that there was not a real piper among them.

A SECOND DAY OF FROGS went by and the roadways were thronged with green. Beds were slimed. Kitchen floors uncrossable. The school yard was a mass of undulating froggery.

The locals began to pack up and move—slowly, because the one highway into the village was covered with both frogs and persons from the media trying to get in. The news organizations, at least, were delighted with the green plague.

"Maybe that will get us a piper," the mayor said to the council after one particularly grueling interview with CNN. And even the thin man had to agree.

And then down the side of Harlingberg Mountain, which being quite steep was relatively frogless, came a drummer. He was a tall, skinny, scruffy man with legs like a stork's. His clothes resembled a personal rummage sale: a green jacket that had once had some sort of emblem on the sleeve; dark pants that were neither black nor blue but somewhere in between; and a white shirt that had certainly seen better days, and probably a better night or two, for it was the tattered remnant of a fancy dress outfit. The drummer had been only partially successful in tucking his shirttails into the pants and one side hung down, obscuring the right-hand pocket, which was just as well as the pocket was no longer there. A pair of granny glasses were perched on his rather prominent nose and made his eyes seem to bulge, rather like those of *Trichobatrachus robustus*. He had a green swatch of cloth tied around his forehead, which did not succeed in keeping his scraggly yellow hair out of his mouth.

A bongo drum was strapped to the tattered man's back and he was carrying a bodhran, a Gaelic hand drum that is played in the best Irish bands.

Once he made his way down the mountainside and found himself right at the town gates, the tattered man marched on his long stork legs through the green swale of frogs, banging all the while on his bodhran. Unaccountably, the frogs opened a path for him, then fell in line behind, hopping feverishly in 4/4 time to keep up with his long strides.

He marched right up the stairs and into the town hall, marking time with the drum. Pushing aside the green invaders, clerks and secretaries opened their doors to stare at him.

"The mayor?" he cried, over the sound of his drum.

Two secretaries and the assistant in charge of weddings, funerals, and bank holidays pointed to the council room door.

Without losing a beat, the drummer stork-legged into the room with his hopping parade behind.

The mayor and council were once again hard at work arguing, but when they saw the drummer and what followed him in two precise lines, they stopped.

"Welcome indeed," said the mayor. "A drummer will do. Name your price." He really knew how to get to the point.

"A bag of gold bullion and a twice yearly gig at the amphitheater," said the tattered drummer. "For me and my band."

The mayor pulled out a piece of paper, swatting away a large guppyi frog from the pen drawer as he did so.

"It's from the Solomon Islands," remarked the thin councilor, pointing to the large frog. The mayor ignored him.

Pen in hand, the mayor asked the drummer, "What is the name of your band?"

"Frog," said the drummer. "Formerly known as Prince."

"Figures," said the mayor. He began to write.

"We'll want guarantees and merchandise rights as well," said the drummer. "And the ability to do a video of the concert intercut with frames from the frog parade."

"Done," said the mayor. He knew better than to argue. Or to go back on his promise. The town legend had taught him that much.

They both signed the paper and then the mayor had one of his secretaries run off copies in triplicate. The councilors put their own signatures in the margins and the mayor handed the drummer a bag of gold. He had, in his own way, done his homework.

The drummer carefully lifted his shirttail, tucked his copy of the agreement in his right pocket, and turned. Smiling, he began drumming in earnest on the bodhran; it was a rhythm in 5/8 time.

The frogs hopped about, forming two straight lines behind him.

Then they all marched out the door, down the steps, along the road, through the village gates, up over Grossmutter Mountain, and were gone, followed by the eager media.

Every last frog left behind the drummer.

For good.

Or for bad.

It depends on how you feel about frogs.

BACK AT THE COUNCIL ROOM only the thin councilor had noticed that the signed contract the drummer put in his missing pocket had floated down onto the floor. Surreptitiously he picked it up and stuck it in his own pants, under the belt, for safekeeping. He knew how short memories were—for plagues and for promises. He ran against the mayor at the next election.

"We will not go from one plague to another!" was his rallying cry. The villagers knew what he meant. Frogs were one thing. A little bit of slime here, a pond full of tadpoles there. Rock-and-roll fests, however, were another: farmyards destroyed, garbage everywhere, and any number of hippies staying on in the village forever. It had happened to a dozen towns on the other side of the mountain.

The thin man won the election overwhelmingly. No one seemed to remember the tale of the piper and the rats when in the voting booth, except for the loud mayor.

"We must not break our promise," he warned.

"What promise?" retorted the thin man, patting the paper under his belt surreptitiously.

The mayor could not convince the voters that history and story have more in common than five letters. He lost in a landslide.

In the fall all the children in the village over the age of fourteen left in a school bus for a rock concert in the next town over the mountain. There was a group called Forever Green that was currently popular. The drummer was known to be toadally awesome.

Only the youngest three children ever returned. They said the others had found their little mountain village stifling. They said the others complained that there were no jobs for them except as tour guides. They said the others wanted to see the world.

The three who came back mentioned that the band had needed roadies.

"You mean toadies," thundered the ex-mayor. It was the line that would carry him back into politics. Into the winner's circle.

And into story.

If not into history.

A Boy and His Frog

BY DAVID LUBAR

• • •

I GUESS I WAS ABOUT FIVE WHEN I GOT Jumparoony. MY young and tender age explains the stupid name. What does a five-year-old know about naming pets? Dad found the tiny frog in the backyard after a heavy rainstorm. Nobody expected him to last long. Especially when he was being taken care of by a little kid. Actually, at first it didn't even look like I'd get to keep him.

"You aren't letting that slimy thing in my house," Mom said, making a face like she'd bitten into a caterpillar.

"Oh, come on," Dad said, "the kid needs a pet."

They argued for a while. From what I remember, the discussion leaped quickly off the subject of the frog and bounced into other areas like Dad's love of bowling and Mom's shopping habits. I never did understand the rules grown-ups used when they argued about stuff. But the end result worked out fine for me.

Once Dad had talked Mom into letting me keep the frog, he warned me not to get upset if the frog croaked. Well, he didn't say it that way, and if he had I wouldn't have gotten the joke, but I remember him explaining that frogs usually didn't last as long as cats or dogs.

The thing is, this frog must not have known that he was supposed to die. He just kept on living. And he kept on growing. Within a year, he'd grown to about the size of a baseball, except of course a baseball doesn't have legs. Or bulging eyes. But if you imagined him rolled up, that's about the size he'd have been.

I really didn't have a clue why he did so well. Maybe I was just good at taking care of pets. Mom says everyone has gifts. I guess I had a special touch with animals. That's the only way I can explain things.

I've had Jumpy—that's what I call him these days—for almost five years now, and during that time, he kept on growing. From the size of a baseball, he went to the size of a softball. At that point, I could still pick him up without any trouble, but parts of him would spill over the sides of my hand.

Then he swelled up to the size of a bowling ball. I started needing two hands to lift him. Once he reached the size of a basketball, I definitely needed both hands. He felt like one of those extra large water balloons.

He was eating a lot, too. I guess you need plenty of food when you're growing that much. It wasn't a problem at first. He did a great job keeping the house free of flies. As long as he stayed inside, there was nothing to worry about. But he got out through the kitchen window one morning and headed straight into the yard next door. Our neighbor, Mrs. Munswinger, used to have five Chihuahuas. Now she has four.

It was an amazing thing to see. Those five annoying little dogs—looking a lot like nervous rats—were huddled together barking at Jumpy. He just sat there calmly for a moment, then he flicked out his tongue and snatched one of the dogs. *Slurp.* The Chihuahua went flying through the air so fast it didn't even have time to let out more than a little yip of surprise before it disappeared headfirst down Jumpy's wide mouth. Its curled tail vanished last, passing through Jumpy's closing lips like a dangling strand of spaghetti.

I dashed over and tried to scoop up my frog. I really couldn't lift all of him off the ground, but I was able to get enough of a grip so I could slide him back toward our yard. Beneath my left hand, I thought I could feel something kicking weakly in his stomach, but I wasn't sure and I really didn't want to think about it. The four surviving dogs just sat there shivering. It was the only time I'd seen them go quiet. I realized it was sort of unfair to say they'd looked like rats. Rats are a lot cuter.

I dragged Jumpy back to the house. Once we got inside, he followed me up the steps to my room. "We're in big trouble," I told him. "There's got to be a law against eating Chihuahuas."

He looked back at me, blinked a couple times, then let out a small burp. Apparently, he wasn't concerned.

Fortunately, Mrs. Munswinger never caught on. She cried and wailed

about her missing darling, her poor dear Mibsey who was lost and gone forever, but she never cast a suspicious eye in my direction.

The next time Jumpy got loose, I caught him right before he hopped into the yard on the other side. That would have been a disaster. Mrs. Hildegarde runs this day care thing in her house, and there are usually a half dozen babies crawling around the yard, eating handfuls of dirt and stabbing at each other with sticks. Most of them are bigger than a Chihuahua, but they're still pretty small.

"This can't go on," I told Jumpy.

He looked at me with that frog expression that seems wise and silly at the same time.

"I have to release you back into the wild. That's the right thing to do." I'd been watching a lot of movies on the Disney Channel, so I knew all about setting wild animals free. I took a deep breath. It wasn't going to be easy. "I'll miss you, buddy."

I led Jumpy to the garage and dragged out my old wagon. He was just too big and squishy for me to lift. "Come on, boy, get in," I said, patting the wagon and trying to sound like we were about to have an adventure.

"Come on. Good boy."

He jumped right up and settled into the bottom of the wagon like a bucketful of pudding. I pulled him along the driveway and out to the sidewalk.

"My word, what is that?" Mrs. Munswinger asked as I walked past her front porch.

I glanced down at the wagon. Jumpy's eyes were closed and his legs were tucked underneath his body, so it really was hard to see any shape. "Mom's cleaning out the fridge," I said. "This was in the back. Want some?"

"No!" She turned pale and backed away from me, holding her hands out like she'd seen a monster.

I headed off. It was a long way to Bear Creek Swamp. I ran into a couple more people, but they just stared at the wagon and didn't ask any questions. When I got to the swamp, I said, "Come on, Jumpy, here's your new home."

He just sat there. Finally, I tipped the wagon over and spilled him onto the ground.

"See ya . . . ," I said. That was all I could manage to choke out. I took one last look at him, then turned and ran off, pulling the wagon behind me.

I missed him. It would be hard to imagine that any kid ever had a better frog. But there were just too many small dogs and little children in the neighborhood. Things would have gotten out of hand.

IT WAS ABOUT TWO YEARS LATER when I first heard folks discussing the sudden drop in the bird population in Bear Creek Swamp.

After that, it was rabbits and squirrels. A couple years later, most of the deer vanished. There were a lot of theories. Everyone tried to explain it. None of the explanations made much sense, but the plain fact was that there was a lot less wildlife than people thought there should be. Once, the area had been filled with deer. Now, a deer was a rare sight.

I realized that things were on their way to getting out of control. Once the deer were gone, Jumpy would probably start on the bears—Bear Creek Swamp wasn't given that name for no reason. But once the bears were gone, along with the rest of the wildlife, I could just imagine Jumpy wandering out of the swamp and into some place where there were lots of people.

I had to try to restore the natural order of things. I couldn't let Jumpy wipe out all life in the swamp. But I didn't want to do anything to hurt him. There had to be another way. He'd started out eating flies. Maybe that was the answer. If I'd raised one giant pet, I figured I should be able to raise another. So I poured a blob of honey on a piece of paper and put it down in the backyard. Then I waited with a jar until some flies landed.

I snuck up on the flies, slammed down the jar, and caught a bunch of them on the first try. I brought them up to my room and started taking care of them. I guess flies aren't supposed to live very long, either. But these did. And they grew.

One fly, especially, started getting real big real fast. I named her Buzzella. Okay, I may have gotten older, but I still stunk at naming pets.

After a week, Buzzella was as big as a bumblebee. In two weeks, she was the size of a sparrow. In a month, she was as large as a vulture. I kept her in an old birdcage I'd found in the basement.

I'll say one thing—as much as a kid is supposed to love his pets, I'd be the first to admit that a fly that size was about as ugly as anything I'd ever seen. And I had a hard time looking her in the eyes. Every time I did, I'd see a million reflections of my guilty face. I felt guilty because I was raising her for one purpose—she and her friends were going to be frog food.

After three months, I took Buzzella and the rest of the flies out to the swamp. I set them loose and watched as they flew off in between the trees. All I could do now was hope that they'd produce lots more flies.

I guess it worked.

It's been three years since I set the flies loose. The wildlife made a comeback. But people don't go into Bear Creek Swamp anymore. After the first few reports of giant flies, everyone learned to stay away. At least the trouble hasn't spread. Whatever is happening, it's just happening in the swamp. So far.

As for me, I'm happy that the flies haven't gotten out of control. Everything is back in balance. My life would be perfect right now except for one tiny thing. Well, actually, a lot of tiny things. Yesterday, for my birthday, my dad gave me an ant farm. I have a funny feeling those four dogs next door aren't out of danger yet.

In the Frog King's Court

BY BRUCE COVILLE

• • •

DENNIS JUGGARUM WAS SQUATTING AT THE EDGE OF Bingdorf's Swamp when he spotted the five-legged frog. The sight made him recoil in fear and disgust. Yet he found he couldn't tear his gaze away.

Despite his revulsion, Dennis decided to catch the thing—partly because he was fascinated by it, partly because he wanted to show it to Mr. Crick, his biology teacher. They had been discussing mutations just a week or two earlier; maybe he could get some extra credit for bringing this one in.

To his surprise, the frog's lopsided condition did nothing to slow it down. Extra leg flapping at its side, the creature easily leaped away before he could lay hands on it.

"Drat!" muttered Dennis. He cursed mostly out of habit, since he wasn't completely sure he wanted to touch the thing anyway. Part of him—not his brain, but something deep in his gut—feared that whatever had caused the mutation might be catching.

That concern didn't stop Dennis from returning to the swamp the next day. Of course, he had gone there nearly every day for the last six years. He liked the swamp, felt oddly at home there—certainly more at home than he ever did in school, where some oaf was always ready to tease him about his odd looks.

He had long ago given up complaining to his mother about the teasing. "What nonsense!" she would scoff. "You're a *very* handsome boy, Dennis." Which, oddly enough, he knew to be almost true. All he needed, as he had told his friend Eric, was eyeball reduction surgery.

But in the swamp he could forget about his looks, about school, about teasing, about everything that bugged him in his daily life. The only thing he couldn't ignore was the sight of old man Bingdorf's chemical factory rising in the distance—the single blot on an otherwise beautifully untamed view.

This afternoon, though, he had come for a more specific purpose than to simply lose himself in the buzz and pulse of life that surrounded him whenever he entered the swamp. This afternoon he wanted to see if he could spot the mutant again.

Squatting a few feet from the murky water, holding himself motionless, Dennis cast his glance in all directions then gasped. Less than three feet to his right crouched a frog with an extra set of eyes growing on its back.

When they blinked at him, he cried out and stumbled backward.

He decided against trying to catch this one.

"Couldn't sneak up on it anyway," he muttered. "Darn thing would see me no matter which direction I came from!"

THAT NIGHT DENNIS told his mother about the mutated frogs.

"I've been reading about that problem in other places," she said, sounding concerned. "They're pretty sure it's caused by chemical pollution in the water. Around here, it would have to come from the Bingdorf factory. Not that old man Bingdorf would care. He'd sell his own children if he thought he could get a decent price for the chemicals they were made of."

The next day she bought a huge plastic filter to put on their kitchen faucet. And she made Dennis start carrying bottled water to school. It was embarrassing, but better than the thought of having three-eyed children when he grew up.

She also forbade him to visit the swamp.

Though Dennis rarely rebelled against a parental order, he couldn't resist the thrilling weirdness of what he had seen. So two days later he went back. The truth was, he would have gone back even without the lure of the mutants. The swamp was simply too important to his peace of mind for him to abandon it so easily.

That afternoon Dennis saw a frog that had an extra foot growing out of each side. He gathered his courage to try to catch it—partly because Mr. Crick had indeed promised him extra credit if he could bring one of the mutants to class, but also because he felt some strange compulsion to hold the creature. Creeping forward, Dennis cupped his hands, ready to bring them down over the frog.

Before he could make his move, the frog leaped away.

Caught up in the chase, Dennis splashed into the swamp after it.

Aside from the fact that it would make his mother angry, going into the water didn't seem dangerous. He had waded into the swamp plenty of times before and he knew it was less than two feet deep in this area.

At least, it had never been more than two feet deep in the past. To his surprise, he now found himself up to his thighs in water.

Even worse, his feet were stuck in the muddy bottom.

No, worse than stuck. He was sinking!

Quicksand! was his first thought. *I've stumbled into quicksand!*

Then something else happened, something so appallingly weird that it drove even the thought of quicksand from his mind. He saw a virtual army of deformed frogs swimming toward him. Dennis cried out in horror as the little monstrosities clambered onto his shoulders, then his head. The clammy flesh of their bellies pressing against the skin of his face drove him mad with fear. They seemed to be weighing him down, pushing him into the soft, sucking bottom of the swamp.

Dennis's terrified screams were cut off as his head went under the surface. The muck—well past his thighs now, nearly to his waist—was holding him, clutching him. Wild with terror, Dennis flailed his arms, churning the water like a propeller.

It did no good.

He opened his eyes. Through the dimly lit water, green and murky, he saw that the swarm of frogs was growing thicker, more dense. Hundreds—no, *thousands* of frogs were swimming closer, trying to push him deeper into the swamp.

Choking on his own terror, Dennis continued his descent into the muddy bottom. The ooze, more terrifying than mere water, crept up his neck. When he felt it on his chin he opened his mouth to scream again. A frog slipped inside. Revolted, he spit it out and clamped his lips shut.

The muck crept past his mouth, beyond his nose.
Finally it closed above his head.

WHEN DENNIS WOKE he was lying facedown on a patch of damp grass. Insects buzzed around him. Under their music he heard the song of frogs—the trill of spring peepers, the tenor tones of the small frogs he used to catch in the swamp, the deep baritone of great bulls. He rolled over, then yelped in fear.

Instead of the distant blue sky, he saw above him a vast expanse of muddy brown, seemingly no more than a few hundred feet away. Directly overhead the brown was replaced by a murky green circle. Dim light filtering through the circle made him wonder if it was really the bottom of the swamp.

Turning from the oppressive "sky," he saw tree-sized mushrooms all around him—a fungal forest that looked fascinating, yet dangerous.

He took a deep breath. The air was damp, but pleasant.

Dennis pushed himself to his feet, his terror at this strange place balanced by the pleasure of finding himself still alive.

"Or maybe I am dead after all," he muttered, wondering if this was what happened when you died.

"No, you're quite fine," replied a deep, throaty voice.

Turning, Dennis saw a frog sitting about five feet away. It was the biggest frog he had ever seen—bigger, even, than any he had ever read about. Easily three feet long, it had bulging eyes that looked like bloated Ping-Pong balls.

"Who are you?" asked Dennis nervously.

"Your guide."

"Guide?"

"Just follow me," croaked the frog. "The king wants to see you."

"Sure," said Dennis, who had now decided that if he wasn't dead he must be crazy. "No problem."

"Good," said the frog. It turned and took three long leaps toward the mushroom forest.

"Wait!" cried Dennis.

The frog—who either didn't hear, or didn't care—continued leaping forward. Not wanting to be left behind, Dennis scrambled to catch up with it.

THE PATH WAS LIGHTLY WORN, and could only be seen by looking carefully. It wound through the giant mushrooms, curving like a snake as it led up and down the low hills. At some point, Dennis wasn't sure when, the oppressively low "sky" was replaced by a normal, decently distant one.

The only problem was that it was bright green.

The sun, or whatever they called the glowing ball that lit the sky here, was green too—the light green of early spring grass.

Dennis wanted to question his guide. But though the huge frog never got out of sight, it always managed to stay far enough ahead that Dennis wasn't able to talk to it.

The mushroom forest gave way to an open grassland dotted with more ponds than Dennis could count. He saw other frogs in the distance, some as large as the one guiding him, a few even larger. They seemed not to notice him, though, or if they did, not to wonder what he was doing here.

On the far side of the grassland was a swamp.

"Awesome," whispered Dennis. For though it was like the swamp at home in some ways, here the ferns grew as tall as trees and the lily pads were the size of carpets. The dragonflies that buzzed through the air had wings as long as Dennis's arms and eyes like living jewels.

Following his guide, Dennis tiptoed along strips of squishy land and crossed murky areas on chains of grassy hummocks. They came, at last, to a pair of towering willows. Growing about ten feet apart, the trees formed a natural doorway.

The guide frog stopped directly in front of the arching willows. When Dennis finally caught up it croaked, "Beyond these trees lies the court of King Urpthur, Lord of All Frogs. Be courteous and respectful when you greet him."

"But why—"

The frog held up its front feet. "The king will tell you what he wants you to know."

Dennis sighed. The question he *really* wanted answered was "Am I dead, crazy, or simply dreaming?" But since "crazy" was a distinct possibility, even if he got an answer it might be nothing but a product of his imagination.

Taking a deep breath, he stepped between the willows, then cried out in delight.

On the far side of the trees stretched a courtroom of elegant beauty. Though it had no walls, its boundaries were clearly marked by stems of mushroom and fern. Growing far straighter here than anywhere else he had seen them, the mushrooms and ferns formed a series of alternating green and beige pillars. The caps of the mushrooms spread like giant umbrellas, while the fern fronds curled high above the court to create a lacy green roof.

In the center of the court shimmered a long pond filled with water lilies, their soup-bowl-sized blossoms displaying a thousand shades of pink, yellow, and white.

Arrayed along the sides of the pond, standing on their hind legs and chatting casually, were dozens of frogs, most of them taller than Dennis. Many wore hats and capes and had swords buckled about their waists.

At the far end of the pond, sitting on an ornate throne carved directly into the giant trunk of a living willow, was King Urpthur. His golden crown was studded with emeralds. A scarlet cape hung from his shoulders. The long green fingers of his right hand curled around a golden scepter. Next to the throne was a gong, suspended from a willow frame.

The court fell silent when Dennis entered. All eyes—and big eyes they were, round and goggling—turned to him.

"Come forward," croaked the king, motioning to Dennis.

Dennis did as he was asked. But when he reached the edge of the pond he stopped, uncertain. Was he supposed to wade through it, or pick his way around it?

One of the nearest frogs, seeing his confusion, gestured to the side of the pond. Looking more carefully, Dennis saw a faint path on the grassy bank. He gave the frog who had pointed it out a grateful look. The frog nodded in acknowledgment.

As Dennis walked around the pond he tried not to stare at the frogs—though he could tell that *they* were studying him with care.

At the far side of the pond the path curved around to bring him directly in front of the king. Dennis paused, uncertain of what to do next. Finally, remembering his guide's warning to "be courteous and respectful," he made an awkward bow.

King Urpthur smiled, which pretty much split his face in half. "Greetings, Dennis. Welcome to my court. Please accept my apologies for the frightening way we brought you here. It is difficult to transport a human to Froglandia—and getting more difficult as the years go by. We only brought you now because of the extreme danger in which we find ourselves."

"The mutated frogs," guessed Dennis out loud. Immediately he wondered if he should have spoken without being asked, and if his words would offend.

But the king merely nodded. "The mutations," he repeated, looking grave. "They are extremely worrisome."

"I agree," said Dennis. "But what do they have to do with me? It's not like I'm a scientist or a politician or anything. I'm just a kid. There's nothing I can do."

"You are a youngster, to be certain," replied the king. "However, you are also one of us."

"I beg your pardon?"

"Granted."

Dennis blushed. "I mean, I don't understand."

"Oh. Oh, I see!" The king began to laugh, a deep, rich, chug-a-rumming. The court joined in, until the result was almost deafening, a percussion concert of croaking.

"As I was saying," said the king, after he recovered from his mirth, "you are part of the frog family."

Dennis was finding it harder to be courteous and respectful.

The king, seeing the doubt on his face, said, "Your nineteenth great-grandfather on your mother's side was what is sometimes called a frog prince. There is often a misunderstanding about this in the old tales. In this case, the princess who kissed the frog was *not* turning an enchanted human back into his own form. She was turning one of my own ancestors (Great-Uncle Hopgo, to be precise—we royal frogs have quite long lives) into a human! Silly of Unkie to give up Froglandia, and his lifespan, for a mere human. But love does that to frogs."

The king blinked his huge eyes twice, seemingly in regret for his great-uncle's foolishness.

"Anyway," he continued. "The point is that you, Dennis, have a small but still significant component of frog blood within you, waiting to assert itself. This explains, by the way, why you have been attracted to swamps all your life."

"But—"

"Oh, don't try to deny it," said the king, waving his hand. "We've watched you gaze longingly into our murky waters. We've listened to your sighs. Can you deny that when you stand at the edge of the swamp something in your blood responds to the muck, and the murk cries out to you: 'Home. That's *home!*' "

Dennis stared at the king in astonishment. Speaking very slowly, he said, "You're telling me that I'm part frog?"

"Yes. A relative, in fact. Lovely news, isn't it?"

Dennis gulped, and hoped that his eyes weren't bulging too much.

"You're not the only distant cousin we have wandering around, of course," continued the king. "But you are the only one who happened to be close to a swamp at the moment. After all, we can't just go hopping into the city and haul people off the streets." He chuckled at the thought, the sound reverberating in his enormous throat.

"What is it, exactly, that you want me to do?" asked Dennis uneasily.

The king's tongue flicked out and snagged a passing insect the size of a small bird. "Sorry, reflex action. I usually try not to eat in front of guests. Now, where were we? Oh, yes. What you can do for us. Well, as you saw at the swamp, my subjects are suffering disastrous effects from the chemicals being leaked into the water. Frogdom has many levels, of course, and at the moment it is only the smallest of my people who are suffering—

the ones tied most closely to your world. But that which happens to the least of my subjects is of concern to me. Am I not their king? What I want you to do is go to the people causing the pollution and make them stop!"

"They won't listen to me. I told you, I'm just a kid."

"They'll listen if you come to them as a frog."

Cold fear prickled along Dennis's neck. Yet at the same time a small voice at the back of his brain began chugging in delight at the idea. His own voice was less willing to function. When he finally did manage to speak, the words came out in a whisper. "You want me to become a frog?"

"Absolutely!" cried the king, leaping to his feet. "I want you to terrify these despoilers of our waters. I want you to appear as the righteous avenger of all frogdom. I want you to hop into their hearts as a symbol of the wrath of nature that will rend them from limb to limb if they persist in their evil ways. I want you, Dennis, to become a crusading frog of doom!"

"You want me to become a frog," repeated Dennis, his voice still little more than a whisper.

"Oh, not permanently," said the king, airily waving a long green hand. "You're not built for it, long term. But just as tadpoles transform themselves into frogs, you have the bloodlines to do the same thing. You just need a little . . . prodding."

"What kind of prodding?" asked Dennis. This was out loud. In his mind he was saying, *Don't panic. It's only a dream!*

The king reached out with his scepter and struck the gong that hung next to his throne. It made a clang like the croak of a metallic frog.

"Yeah, yeah, yeah," said a hoarse voice, the words seeming to come from the ground itself. "I'll be there in a minute."

A sudden hiss of steam beside the throne made Dennis step back. The ground, which had seemed solid, began to bubble. The steam gathered into a swirling cloud, then turned green. An instant later it vanished, leaving in its place a stoop-shouldered old frog with wire-rimmed glasses perched on his nose. He wore a dark green robe covered with stars and moons. Cupped between his green fingers was a wooden goblet that had lilies carved around its stem. Steam, or smoke, or something flowed over the edge of the goblet and fell to the ground like mist, where it continued to curl about his webbed feet until he appeared to be standing in a small cloud.

He looked at Dennis with something that resembled a smile. "Nice entrance, huh, kid?"

"It was amazing," said Dennis quite honestly. "Who are you?"

The old frog sighed. "Don't tell me you never heard of Murklin the Mudgician. Forget it. I don't wanna know. No one teaches kids anything these days. Here, drink this."

He extended the steaming goblet to Dennis, who stared at it in horror.

"What happens if I do?" he whispered, his hands still at his sides.

"It will release your inner frog," said the king happily. "Make the destiny written in your blood clear for all to see. Bring your great—"

"Shut up, Urpthur," said Murklin.

The king blinked, but fell silent.

Dennis continued to stare at the goblet, which was burping and blurping with little pops of muddy-looking liquid.

"What if I don't want to?" he asked.

An angry murmur rose behind him. "Traitor," he heard low voices croak. "Ingrate!"

The king raised a hand. "We will not force you, Dennis," he said, staring past him to silence the angry courtiers. "But if you do refuse, you will forever bear the knowledge that you abandoned kin and king in their hour of need. You will know you let fear, not courage, rule your heart. You will forever remember yourself as one not willing to shed your skin for a greater cause."

"But I don't *want* to be a frog!"

"Part of you already is," replied the king reassuringly. "A small part, granted. But part of you nevertheless. Besides, it's not permanent. You'll only be a frog sometimes."

"When?"

"The night before and the night after the full moon are what we call 'frog moons.' On those sacred nights you can go in your froggy glory to confront the villains who are poisoning my subjects. Oh, Dennis, Dennis—think of it! To how many men is it given to find the secrets hidden in their blood, to wear two shapes, to live two lives? To how many men is it given to speak truth to power, to be a voice for their people? How many, how many are allowed to croak for the good of others?"

Inspired by the king's words, Dennis reached at last for the goblet. It was warm between his hands. He gazed into it. The greenish brownish brew, bubbling and popping, looked like a miniature swamp.

"This is my destiny," he told himself. "And besides, it's only a dream, so who cares?"

He lifted the cup to his lips. It smelled of the swamp and of wildness and of magic. The first swallow was difficult, thick and murky. But then the potion took its hold on him. Surrendering himself to it, he drained the cup to the last drop.

The frogs burst into ribbiting cheers as the world swirled green around him.

WHEN DENNIS WOKE, he found himself lying at the edge of the swamp. The hot sun beat down on his face.

Beside him sat a tiny three-legged frog. Dennis reached for it, but the little frog hopped awkwardly into the water.

"What a weird dream," he groaned as he pushed himself to his feet. "I must be coming down with something."

"Where have you been?" growled his mother, when he came through the door. "Dinner was ready half an hour ago!"

"I was out visiting some . . . friends," said Dennis. Then, on a whim, he asked, "Mom, did we ever have any royalty in our family?"

His mother smiled. "Well, according to Gramma Wetzel, your nineteenth great-grandfather on my side was a genuine prince."

Dennis gaped at her in horror.

"Den? Is something wrong?"

"No," he said. "Nothing. I just don't feel all that well."

Nothing. It had to be nothing. He clung to that thought.

Even so, when he went to his room after supper, he opened his window and pushed up the screen—just in case he needed to get out later on.

Eventually he fell into a fitful sleep, marked by dreams that were strange and soggy.

He awoke just past midnight. The moon was shining through his window. As he remembered from the night before, it was round and nearly full—nearly, but not quite.

A frog moon.

Suddenly Murklin's potion began its strange work. Dennis's eyes began to bulge. He grabbed for his ears. Too late! They were shrinking—or maybe pulling into his head. He slid his hands upward. His hair! It was disappearing into his clammy skin.

Looking down, he saw his legs growing longer, stronger, and greener as his feet stretched and his toes became connected by a thin membrane.

He was engulfed by a wave of terror so intense that he feared he might croak.

An instant later the terror was replaced by pain—a rending pain that seared him from head to toe.

And then, in a moment, it was over.

Staggering to his feet, Dennis found that despite having become a frog he was still his regular height, maybe even a bit taller. Clearly he was the kind of frog he had seen at the king's court. He held his hands before him, marveling at his long, green fingers and the webbing that stretched between them.

A cool night breeze lifted the curtains, carrying with it the odor of the swamp. Dennis found the smell irresistible. In only a moment he had scrambled over the sill and onto the lawn, where he dropped to jumping position.

The cool, dew-laden grass felt sweet against his flat white belly. He blinked twice, took another deep breath of the moist air. Then—without really thinking about it—he unleashed the power of his mighty legs.

The force of his leap frightened him and his heart began to hammer as he hurtled into the air and across the yard.

Too high! he thought in terror. *I'm going too high!*

Yet when he landed and realized he had survived the leap, he felt a surge of joy. *It's almost like flying!* thought Dennis. Flexing his legs again, he bounded joyfully around the lawn, leaping higher and higher in the darkness.

A chorus of tiny peeps brought him to a halt.

Coming toward him, leaping through the night as if the entire field behind the house was starting to percolate, were his . . . well, his cousins;

hundreds and thousands of frogs, tiny ones in the lead, larger ones—
though not so large as him, of course—bringing up the rear.

The frog moon floated above them like an enormous silver coin.

His cousins surrounded him, an avenging army of frogdom. The lit-
tlest ones crept forward to stare up at him, their goggling eyes awash
with admiration.

Dennis felt a sense of purpose surge through him. Someone had to
protect these little ones, and he was just the frog to do it.

Taking a deep breath, he puffed out his throat and emitted a sound
that astonished even him, a deep bass note, a trumpet call of warning
that reverberated through the night—the sound of a mighty amphibian who had had enough.

Fire in his froggy eyes, Dennis turned to lead his leaping army toward old man Bingdorf's estate.

Polliwog

BY STEPHEN MENICK

And the Lord said to Moses, "Say to Aaron, 'Stretch out your hand with your rod over the rivers, over the canals, and over the pools, and cause frogs to come upon the land of Egypt!'" —Exodus 8:5

• • •

"It takes a father to know a father's love."

We were bathing in the river, my son and I. He was old enough to bear the chill before the sunrise. I remember standing in the river while he sat on the steps, churning the water with his feet.

"Stop looking at the water and look at your father," I said. "You will never know what my love means until you yourself become a father someday. Do you understand me?"

"Yes."

"Nonsense. Remember this moment. Remember your father talking to you in the river, saying things about a father's love. Things you didn't understand because you were just a little boy."

"Daddy, polliwogs!"

I never could hold his attention.

"Yes, I see them," I said. Three of them wiggled in the water between us. "They could be little fish, couldn't they, with their tails? What will they become?"

"Frogs."

"Someday they'll grow arms and legs, and they'll be frogs. Tell me. Do you think a polliwog can know what it's like to be a frog? To have arms and legs for swimming?"

My son was chasing the polliwogs with his eyes. His name was Tetef, and he loved the old stories of our wonderful Egyptian faith. To bring him back to me, I said, "God or goddess, Tetef?"

"The goddess Hekit."

"That's right," I said. "Hekit, the goddess of all the frogs. The goddess of great change. Of rebirth. Eternal life. What day is today, Tetef?"

"The first day after the Night of Tears, Daddy."

"How can you tell?"

"The river's rising. Isis has been crying."

"Every year at this time," I said, "Isis weeps. Her tears fall from heaven and feed the river, and the river feeds us."

My son was wet and shivering.

"Let's go, Polliwog. Your mother will be angry with me if you catch cold." The servants wrapped him in towels as he came up the steps. The sun rose behind the reeds and sailed through the day.

It has been many thousands of days since then. I am an old man now.

Each morning I still bathe in the river. I go down the steps while the reeds wear the halo of the coming sun. My crocodile watchers go first, watching the reeds, watching for the ripples. One of my watchers died today. The stillness of the dawn was broken by the splash and his cries.

I paused in my bath to look as the others tried to save him. I am always enraptured by these struggles of men with things that are greater than they. I turned to go, and then the river—our Nile, our river of secrets—the river showed me things. A red gloom, the blood of the dying man, passed through the water in front of me, and there was a wiggling of polliwogs.

I hurried indoors. My sandal bearer saw me with my hand to my face. I said I had a mite in my eye. Other servants were waiting, and when they saw my distress they made a move to call for my doctors. I sent them all away. Women and children may weep. Men may weep in front of other men. Even a goddess may shed tears. A Pharaoh, never.

I SHOULDN'T HAVE trusted the magicians.

I knew them from my father's court. We children were afraid of them. They draped themselves in amulets to ward off the spirits with whom they meddled, and the amulets rattled with their approach. They whitened their faces with gypsum and smelled of mummy tars and crocodile dust. They turned my stomach from the start.

Our faith is full of simple joys. A man who can see the sun on the boat of Ra sailing into the west, knowing that it will be borne back on the morning winds after its journey among the stars: a man to whom that daily resurrection is a reminder of the voyage our souls will make someday has no need of magicians' tricks. Upon my father's death and my ascent to the throne, I banished the magicians from my sight.

But a man who has no son is incomplete in this life, and it was my misfortune to have daughters. All my wives gave me daughters. When I was with my wives I prayed to Isis for a son like Horus, a hawk of a man carrying my heart in his talons. I prayed—and had more daughters.

I believed then, and I still believe, that to accept our destinies as they are, remembering that all the wounds of this life will be healed in the hereafter, is the greatest of virtues. But my hunger for a son caused me to put aside that virtuous ideal. I let the magicians back into my midst, into my court. I let them do unspeakable things. I choked on their smoke and retched from their potions. Under the babble of their spells I heard my own voice within me, whispering of my son-to-be.

Tetef was born on a night of the full moon. Great numbers of my subjects held a vigil by the palace arcade, and the air was sweet with the smoke of palm branches. Birth—the coming forth from the shadows of the womb—is an occasion as solemn as it is happy, and as I strode from the birthing place to hold my son aloft before the people, I seemed to have entered that corridor of rushing sounds and wild lights which is said to mark the departure of the soul from the body. The people thundered in jubilation, and on either side of me the priestesses were chanting and shaking their silver rattles. The moon broke into four moons and then seven. Glorious green meteors fell over their reflections in the Nile. This was the work of the magicians, who had come trotting on my heels and were tricking the heavens in a vulgar display of power. They had handed me the thing I had wanted most dearly in the world: but what would be their price? I held my son above my head and felt him arching his back, and I began to fear for him and for me.

EVEN THEN IT WAS TOO LATE, even then the web was being woven, strand by secret strand over the course of time. I have said that there were magicians in my father's court. Long before I was born, a magician had prophesied that among one of our subject peoples, the Hebrews, a dangerous man would arise, a man who would harm our land, our river, even Pharaoh himself. At the time of the prophecy this man was said to be an infant: as a precaution, therefore, my father ordered the killing of all male Hebrew infants—a vast undertaking, as can be imagined. Surely the soldiers left many stones unturned. One of my elder sisters was bathing in the river one morning when her crocodile watchers found a little boat among the reeds, and in that boat was a child who had escaped the sword. In the way of women, my sister took pity on the child, though she should have known better. She swore her servants to secrecy.

So it was that this—this man whose name I cannot force past my lips—this Hebrew was lifted from the water and educated in our court. As a youth he was a passionate student of magic. He proved, indeed, a fine example of why our magicians have always gone to great pains to keep the dark craft from falling into the wrong hands. He showed his true colors when, in a fit of rage, he murdered an Egyptian for striking a Hebrew laborer. He then admitted who he was—a stranger among us—and fled.

It caused great embarrassment in our family. I was a child then, but quite old enough to understand what was going on. My sister was horrified, shamed before my poor father, who had wanted nothing more than to live his last years in peace. The magicians were blamed for failing to see through the impostor's mask. They looked heavenward and read their star-tables and said there was no sign of the Hebrew ever returning to Egypt. The scandal died down with the years, but I, for one, never forgot it, and it fed my distaste for magicians and all things magical.

My father died at the age of eighty. He was buried in the sandstone hills with his gold and his gems and a boat made of cedarwood like the sun-boat of Ra, and I became Pharaoh. I had busy years, wars to wage, cities to build, and yet I was happiest when I was at home with my son beneath my gaze. The best years of my life did not begin the day I was made King of Upper and Lower Egypt and Lord of the Six Cataracts and Seven Mouths of the Nile. My best years began the night Tetef drew his first breath.

During those years there were magicians in my court. I had brought them back because they had given me Tetef. This was not simple gratitude on my part. I am not a simple man, and in my mind was ever the notion that someday the magicians might try to take back what they had given me. Better to keep them close at hand, where they could be watched.

Tetef was seven when my watchers told me that the magicians had become aware of one of their own—another magician—on the banks of the Nile. They could sense his presence, just as jackals can smell other jackals from afar. It was the Hebrew. Like the jackal, shy of humankind, he had been living in the wilderness, the kingdom of silence. The wilderness, as we know, is infested with demons, and our magicians were much too curious about him to send him away as the murderer he was. They wished to see what mastery he had achieved over the forces of the wastelands. They met with him, then they brought him to me, saying there might be a problem.

Time and the elements had not been kind to him. He looked like a raisin with white hair. At his side was another Hebrew—his brother, they told me—acting as his helper. They threw down a wand and stood back as it came to life as a cobra. The thing reared up and hissed at me. There was a clatter of ebony and a pibble-pabble of words of power as our own magicians flung their wands. The floor was writhing with cobras. For a while I lost track of which were ours and which was theirs. One of them swallowed another, then another and another, tossing its head back to gulp each one down like a servant shuffling a pillowcase to get the pillow inside. It was disgusting. When no others remained, it let out an enormous belch. The Hebrew stepped forward and grabbed it—it stiffened into a wand again—and walked out.

If ever there was a time to put an end to it, it was then, at the beginning, when I saw the look in our magicians' eyes. I have never craved power: fate handed it to me. I have never had the desire to frighten or impress others: it was given to me to do so, as my duty. But magicians are devoted to these shallow pursuits, and they hate it when another steals their thunder.

The contest had begun. I allowed it to continue. I didn't like what had just happened in my court. I didn't like this Hebrew. I didn't like his manner. I turned to the magicians and used the words I use countless times every day: "Correct this situation."

Magic for magic. The next trick was to change the waters of our river into blood. The Hebrew and the magicians dueled like swordsmen, dipping their wands into the river until the stink of blood and dead fish was ferocious. It was midsummer and the river was rising. At dawn the next day I took Tetef down to the reeds and told him he couldn't bathe.

"What happened, Daddy?" he said, making a face. He turned away from the blood and held his nose.

I didn't want to frighten him any more than he was already, so I told him that sometimes Isis cried blood instead of water. I told him the blood would go away soon. But the little boy was bewildered and unhappy.

I sent him off to his morning lessons and roared for the magicians. As soon as they saw my mood they wiped the smiles off their faces.

"Pleased with yourselves?" I said.

Their chief, whose name was Morenu, spoke up: a gap-toothed old trickster who'd never done an honest day's work in his life.

"We've done well, Lord."

"Done well?"

"We've demonstrated quite competently, I think, that our magic is as robust as the Hebrew's. Naturally, we admit that the situation is not yet to our complete satisfaction, Lord. But, it's an improvement over the other day."

I paced back and forth without so much as a glance at them. "Tell that to the laborer at noon. Tell it to the baker. Tell him to bake red bread. And then let me see you eat it. Do you know you've got my son scared out of his wits? When will the river be back to normal?"

"It may take perhaps as much as a week, Lord."

"A week?"

"For the spells to wear off."

"Seven days, then. Not one day more, or there'll be blood all right, and it'll come out of you."

Egypt thirsted. The people had to dig trenches around the river to find the sweet water that had seeped into the ground before the spells.

On the seventh day it was over, and I took Tetef down to bathe with me. The river was as clear as our heavens, with lotus petals for stars. I spun Tetef around so that his toes scissored the water—he always liked that. After his tutors came for him I paused by the reeds, drinking from my cupped hands, thinking about a thousand things. Frogs went skipping through the water between my legs. I thought of Tetef as a father someday, Tetef as Pharaoh, and not for the first time did I wish him a happier Egypt than mine. There were a great many frogs that morning.

Too many. I'd never seen anything like it. I was standing in the water, watching it turn green, when I lost my footing in the mud and the river vomited a huge jelly of live frogs.

The upchuck swept me onto the land. The river heaved another blob that shivered and shattered into frogs.

"Call the magicians!"

It was like the first blast of a sandstorm, when the sand starts blowing into the house and the servants scramble to shut doors and windows in the vain hope of halting the invasion. A servant fell to one knee amid a flurry of frogs and said the magicians were busy at the moment.

"Doing what?"

"Doing battle with the Hebrews, Lord."

"Daddy! Daddy!"

Trailed by his tutors, their arms full of slates and papyrus rolls, Tetef came running down the hall laughing, a frog in each hand.

"Frogs!"

"I can see that, Tetef."

"Frogs and frogs!"

"I know, I know."

"Frogs and frogs and more and more frogs!"

The house had gone mad. One old servant of ours, a large woman, fell on her face grabbing a single frog as a hundred other frogs jumped in front of her and crisscrossed like green latticework, and Tetef's giggling tickled my ears and melted my heart. I picked him up. We watched the servants and laughed together.

"Froggies and froggies, Daddy!"

Any father who has ever held his cheerful son, held him and looked into the sparkle in his eyes, knows what I was blessed to see just then.

"The goddess is laughing, Polliwog," I said. "The goddess is laughing. We should laugh with her. You!"

A servant was wading among the frogs in the lily pond in our foyer.

"Yes, Lord?"

"Bring me this Hebrew. I want to talk to him."

I HAD BEEN TOLD the Hebrew had his own god, that he had met this god in the wilderness. Other religions interest me. Although I have never found a faith as comforting as ours, I enjoy sitting down with foreigners and hearing about their gods and views of the hereafter. I did this with the Hebrew. My motives were practical. Rather than continue to fight fire with fire—which seemed to me rather unimaginative—I thought it would make sense to rid myself of the man by subtler means.

He entered my presence without greeting me, sat down and stared at the floor. I don't think he looked at me twice throughout. It was an absurd little interview, the Hebrew sulking like an adolescent, the two of us swatting frogs and trying to make ourselves heard over the croaking.

"What's your god's name?"

"No name."

"You must call him something. What do you call him?"

He shook his head. I took this to mean that the name was a word of power and not to be shared.

"Well then, what does he look like?"

"Doesn't look like anything."

"How do you represent him?"

"We don't."

"Where is he?"

"Nowhere in particular."

"I thought he was in the wilderness. My spies tell me—"

The Hebrew looked up.

"Don't get upset," I said. "Spies are a necessity. How else would we learn things? They tell me your god lives in a bush."

"No."

"But that's where you met him. He spoke to you out of a fiery bush. If he wasn't in the bush, where was he? Where is he now?"

"Everywhere. Nowhere."

"A wind god. A spirit of the air."

He snorted.

"Tell me what you want from me," I said.

"Let my people go."

"You know that's out of the question. Help me understand what you believe, then we'll see about the rest. What does your god have planned for you?"

"A land of milk and honey."

"We have something like that in our religion. We believe that when we die—"

"Not when we die. In this life."

"This life lasts but a moment," I said. "It would seem to me that what comes afterward is far more important."

He shrugged. I couldn't get anywhere with him. He kept insisting that I let his people go. I explained as patiently as I could that I was not in the habit of releasing subject peoples.

"Then make an exception," he said.

"If I made an exception for you, I'd have to make an exception for everyone, and that would put me in an impossible position. You have your people to answer to. I have mine."

He hung his head and shook it: "Let my people go." I almost expected him to stamp his foot, but he was already sitting down.

I am not one who gives up easily. However, it had been a long, loud, slimy day. "Get rid of these infernal frogs," I said, "and we'll take a fresh look at this some other time."

The frogs died the next morning. My servants and the people and their servants all went to work gathering them up for burning. The memory of that stench—first the frogs rotting in the sun, then the smoke of the pyres—still makes me sick. I was forced to conduct state business looking like a common gravedigger, with a cloth over my nose. At dusk, when on any other day I would have sipped beer on my balcony, watching the sun dipping behind the pyramids—at dusk, my

Egyptian sky was greasy with the smoke of the frogs. I could not have conceived there was worse to come.

The cycle of terror and destruction which that man brought upon our land is still remembered by Egyptians, so I will not dwell on the details. But there are some parts of the story that have never been told. Shortly after the frog episode, the Hebrew accused me of going back on my word—which was ridiculous, because I had given my word on nothing—and made his first threat, saying he would raise a plague of lice next if I failed to let his people go. In my chilliest tone of voice I thanked him for giving me advance notice of his movements and intentions. Inwardly, I seethed. I do not take well to threats. They make me obstinate. But the last thing I was going to do was let him see into my heart.

I spoke just now of my heart, and I must say that in my heart I was proud of my Polliwog when I saw him frowning at the man like a little Pharaoh. For it was around this time that the Hebrew, accompanied by his brother, began calling on me during my morning plunge in the river with my son. The pair of Hebrews looked at Tetef and whispered to each other.

My generals also came to see me—my men, my comrades-in-arms. We'd fought side by side in the south of Egypt campaign and been bloodied together in the Battle of the Sixth Cataract. Scornful of magic, believers in the sword, my men had been straining like horses to solve the Hebrew problem their way. I held them back. I was never keen on attacking unarmed people, and the Hebrew population appeared to be unarmed. I failed to grasp the magnitude of their invisible weapons, all in the hands of one man.

Meanwhile, the behavior of our Egyptian magicians was chafing at my tolerance. After the Hebrew raised his plague of lice, causing no end of vexation to every man, woman, child, and beast of Egypt, I found the magicians trying to copy the trick, as they'd done with the blood and the frogs. This struck me as the height of foolishness.

"Instead of trying to make more lice," I said, scratching myself like a stable boy, "why don't you make them go away?"

They could do neither, nor could they ward off the afflictions which the Hebrew visited upon us in the days that followed: flies, cattle sickness, boils, hailstorms, locusts. We know the locust all too well in our part of the world. Every now and then the old enemy comes tumbling out of the East singing its shrill song. But these locusts were infinite in number. We could hear them singing before we saw them on the horizon, so massive was the swarm. It was as though a millstone rolled over Egypt, and we were the grain.

I am aware that many of my subjects questioned then the wisdom of their Pharaoh, asking how I could let so much suffering go on, when I could have shaken us all awake from the nightmare. If I could rewrite that sad chapter—if I could hear again my son's laughter as he holds a frog in each hand—I would go to the Hebrew quarter myself and drive every last one of those people out of our country. But the river of time flows only in one direction, and even the gods go downstream with the rest of us. Seldom do we see past the next bend, the next sandbar, the next waterwheel thumping among the reeds. We only know what we know at the time. Here is what was in my mind in those dark days.

We were all equal under the Hebrew's spells, but I suffered deeply in my own way, knowing that I had it in my power to end the agonies of Egypt if only I allowed my spirit to break. Many times it came close to breaking. I remember the time it came closest. After all the other plagues—those maddening blows—we were under the locusts, and from my balcony I couldn't see the pyramids for the swarm. The goddess of night herself cannot hide our pyramids; they stand black against the stars. I stared at the appalling gloom and felt it entering into my soul, and I was about to summon the Hebrew to tell him he had won, when the locust clouds parted for a moment to reveal the eternal form of the Great Pyramid. I thought of the men who had lived and died to build that mountain of stone, that pinnacle of Egypt, that wonder of the world. I thought, or I tried to think, of all they must have endured. Surely we could endure these . . . these insects. Even with the swarm screaming in my ears, my thoughts were very clear to me. I don't know if they will be understood by others. Perhaps it takes a Pharaoh to understand a Pharaoh.

The west wind lifted the locusts away, and we were left with nothing. The swarm had nibbled every leaf, blade of grass, and ear of grain under the Egyptian sun. Fortunately, the royal granaries had been sealed, and the people did not starve. But my spies heard grumblings that the Hebrew was greater than Pharaoh, that Pharaoh was helpless and afraid.

He was. When next the Hebrew raised a storm that blew the sunboat of Ra off course, and there was no dawn: then I began to doubt even our gods. That was when the magicians came to me, their amulets rattling in the dark. I could see only their faces, white with gypsum, floating like moths.

"The locusts, Lord," Morenu said.

"Aren't they gone? Why do you mention them now?"

"We have some of them in jars."

"Destroy them!"

"With all reverence, Lord, we haven't done so. We've kept them for study."

It seemed the magicians had collected a number of the locusts, and in the patterns of the spots on some of the locusts' wings, they had read the name of the demon whom the Hebrew called his god.

"What is the name?"

"Forgive me, Lord, but it would be unwise to speak it."

"Yes, of course," I said, understanding that it was a word of power.

"It is a name that none of us has ever heard before," Morenu said. "A name unknown until this day."

"Look around you. There is no day."

"There will be again, Lord."

I listened. I listened as that little monkey told me of their plan to strike at the Hebrew's source of power. The name of the demon was the key. They were preparing a spell that contained the name, a spell that would send the demon back into the wilderness like the locusts on the west wind. The spell would disarm the Hebrew, make him like any other man, and then I could do with him what I pleased.

"Will it work?" I asked after a moment.

"We're confident that it will."

I'd always supposed that if I ever had to defend Egypt in her darkest hour, it would be with a sword in my hand, or with my feet on my chariot charging into armies, not this way, with a smelly pack of magicians I could barely see. Then again, these were the ones who brought Tetef into the world. Good can come from bad. I said, "See to it."

Their amulets rattled as they left. They went about their preparations, surely the blackest magic ever practiced in a Pharaoh's court. From their chambers came screams. I didn't want to know what

was going on down there. Tetef couldn't sleep. I read to him by lamplight—I read from the Tales of the Ibis and the Ostrich, one of my favorites as a child—until he went limp and I put him in his bed.

For as long as I read to Tetef I seemed to hear only his breathing and the sound of my voice. Later, on my balcony, I heard the first cries arising from the city. Soon came reports of some terrible thing happening in our land.

The loss of our firstborn sons was the final blow to Egypt in the hours before the Hebrews departed. The blow was delivered after the magicians cast their spell against the demonic forces that held our land captive. We still do not know whether the spell was poorly prepared or was simply too weak. We do know that it was repulsed, cast back at us, and the demon took its vengeance.

My generals appeared before me in battle gear bringing word that the Hebrews were on the road to the Red Sea. In green-and-gold armor my men came to find their Pharaoh. All they found was another father, grieving over his firstborn son. I had taken Tetef down to the river to bathe him in the new dawn. There was a bloom of red from his nose. Polliwogs wiggled through it.

It has been said that the expedition against the Hebrews was suicidal from the start, that I should never have allowed it. I did not allow it. When my generals came to me I was incapable of giving an order of any kind. They spoke to me from the steps by the water, but I heard them from a great distance. From a great distance I heard them go away. And from a great distance I heard the trembling messenger tell of the final moments of my army, engulfed as the walls of the sea fell back on them. The loss meant nothing to me. My men, my horses, my chariots were nothing next to my son, my Tetef, my little Polliwog.

Magic is an evil thing. It springs from the smallness and vanity of the heart, and carries too high a price. So that Egypt should never pay such a price again, I had the magicians put to death, and made the practice of magic a crime punishable by death, as it remains to this day.

To those who may still dabble in secret, defying their Pharaoh and his law, I say that there is no greater proof of the perils of the dark craft than the fate of the Hebrew and his people. On the other side of the sea he led them into the wilderness, the homeland of the demon who had served him. We had reports of their wanderings, deeper and deeper into that labyrinth of red rocks and bewildering echoes, and then the reports dwindled to nothing. It has been nearly forty years now. They have all gone to dust.

The gods have been good to Pharaoh. I have a secondborn son and a third and a fourth, and on the day I die, my eldest will take the throne that was to be for Tetef. I look forward to that day. I can feel it coming. Each morning when I bathe in the river—while the priestesses chant, and the jewels on the arms of the harpists catch the rays of the dawn— I see the sails of the sun-boat of Ra. At the tiller stands Tetef, a grown man, broad-shouldered and smiling, flanked by golden cobras, under the vulture's wings.

Ahem

BY NANCY SPRINGER

• • •

SHASTA WISHED ON A STAR. SHE WISHED FOR A FRIEND.

Her name, *Shasta,* meant "star," which was an extraterrestrially dumb name for her parents to have given her. She was no star. She was thirteen, gawky, she had knees that stuck out, elbows that stuck out, hair that stuck out in all directions, a nose that—in fact, every part of her stuck out except her chest. And her personality. If anybody had told her classmates she was a "star," they would have laughed, if they could even remember who she was.

Nevertheless, she was Shasta and she was allowed to wish on a star. Standing in her small backyard, looking out over the rooftops of the other development houses at a sundown sky murky with sodium vapor lamps, Shasta felt herself starting to shiver—and not just from the October chill. She had never done this before, and she knew she had to be careful: Her wish could come true. She knew this because her golden-eyed godmother had told her so, and Godmother had known everything. If Godmother said the stars were fireflies, in that imperious headmistress tone of hers, why then, fireflies they were. When

Godmother had told Shasta to wish on a star if she wanted anything, Shasta had known that wishes were real. But Godmother had also said that wishes were tricky, so Shasta had saved hers for something important. She had saved it until she felt sure she would not be able to face middle school for even one more day unless she did something.

In the gray-and-orange sky flecked with autumn clouds, only one star showed. Taking a deep breath, Shasta spoke to it.

"Star white, star bright." Shasta hated her own voice, a breath, barely louder than a whisper. No way the evening star could hear her. Nobody ever heard her. "Wish I may, wish I might . . ." Her murmur was lost in the muddy sky.

Maybe Godmother had been teasing?

Maybe. Godmother had been mischievous sometimes. Tricky, like wishes. ". . . wish I might have a friend to make things all right."

Godmother was dead. Over a year now. Shasta missed her.

She missed her a lot.

The evening was getting colder. Shasta hugged herself and watched the sky darken to a muddier orange gray for a moment longer, then sighed, kicked at the half-frozen ground, and turned away, trudging up her crabgrassy yard toward her house. Nothing had happened. Nothing was going to happen—

"Ahem," said a froggy voice close at hand.

Shasta jumped and looked all around, peering in the dusk. What was it, a ghost? There was nobody in the backyard except her—but then she saw. Like a lump on the lawn at her feet, the same color as the crabgrass, sat a large bullfrog.

"Good evening," said the voice.

It was froggy for a reason; it came out of the bullfrog. The frog was speaking. Shasta saw its mouth open. She saw its wet, toothless salmon-colored gums. She saw its sticky yellow tongue thrashing to shape the words. The frog was—

Talking? Frog?

Startled, Shasta stumbled back.

"Don't be a ninny." The frog ogled at her with glistening eyes, puffing itself even larger and more lumpy than before. "You requested a friend? Here I am."

Shasta felt queasy. She always liked to know whether a potential friend was a boy or a girl, and with this frog, she couldn't tell. And she didn't feel like it would be polite to ask. And an instant later she didn't care whether she knew, darn it. She felt so disappointed that her shy voice rose almost to a whisper. "I wanted a *human* friend." Oh, darn, double darn, her wish had come true after all, but it had tricked her. How could this creature be her friend? It was nothing but a frog.

But then she remembered the fairy tales and thought of something that made her blush, feeling suddenly so warm that she could barely speak. She whispered, "Am I, uh, am I supposed to, like, kiss you?"

"A polite kiss would be most welcome," declared the frog. "However, it is cold out here. Take me inside first."

The frog spoke in quite a commanding tone, and Shasta was used to doing as she was told. She crouched and picked up the frog around its squishy middle. Frogs have no ribs, she remembered from having dissected a frog in biology class. No wonder this one squatted like a soggy silk beanbag in her two cupped hands. She took it inside, and, as usual, her mother and father didn't notice as she came in. They did not see the frog. They did not even look up from their *New Yorkers* as she carried it past them and up the stairs.

She set the frog on top of her dresser. With its long back legs sprawling and its throat throbbing, it turned great golden eyes to watch her.

Shasta took a deep breath, closed her eyes, then kissed it.

She opened her eyes. The frog was still squatting there looking back at her. "Boogers," Shasta whispered, one of the worst words she knew, and it was the appropriate
color for the occasion,
too.

"I beg your pardon?"

"Nothing happened."

"Is something sup-
posed to happen?"

Shasta ignored the
question, because she
felt sure that if she an-
swered it she would
end up feeling even
more stupid than she
already did. Stupid and
wretched, so miserable
that she barely no-
ticed the green
duckweedy taste
the frog had left

on her mouth. "I wasted my wish." The soft words slipped out like tears.

"Ahem," said the frog. "I beg to differ."

Stupid frog. "Go away." Shasta knew that nobody ever did what she said, so she turned her back on the frog. Maybe if she didn't look, she would be able to forget that it was still there.

No such luck. She heard scrabbling noises as the frog explored the top of the dresser. "It is unpleasantly dry here," said the frog. "I prefer a wet place."

"So find one," Shasta muttered. She knew she should take the frog back outside and let it go, but phooey on it. Bossy, fat, booger-colored frog. It had told her to take it inside, so now it was inside and it could just live with being dry. Shasta decided that it was no use trying to face the rest of the evening. Even though it was only seven o'clock, she went to the bathroom, brushed her teeth and got herself a drink of water, came back to her room, scowled at the frog, closed the door so her parents wouldn't bother her, and went to bed.

When her alarm clock beeped the next morning, she groaned and swatted it silent, then sprawled without opening her eyes. Another day of middle school. She couldn't stand it, she knew she couldn't, she just wanted to stay in bed and never get up again.

Then she remembered that she had a talking frog.

A talking frog?

She opened her eyes and looked at the dresser. She looked at the door; it was still closed. She sat up and looked at the top of the dresser again. Then she got up and looked all around the room. She looked under her bed, but it wasn't there, either.

Gone.

It must have gotten out somehow. Stupid, squishy frog. Great. Fine. Whatever. So much for her wish. Forget having a friend. She was too much of a loser even to keep a frog as a friend, she had to go to school, and she felt like she was getting a cold. There was a lumpy feeling in her throat.

Walking to meet the school bus, she looked only at the gray asphalt, which matched the gray sky, which matched her mood.

She had no idea how she was going to get through another day.

ON THE BUS, SHASTA sat like a ghost, eyes down, studying the bits of notebook paper lying in the gray grooves of the rubber flooring, not looking at anybody, and she was lucky this morning; everybody was sleepy and nobody noticed her. By walking into school the same way, like a ghost, she managed to make it to her locker and then to home-room without being picked on.

But once she reached homeroom, that was it. Trapped in a classroom with thirty bored kids, she didn't stand a chance.

"Here comes Shasta! What a disasta!" yelled a tall, loud girl sitting on top of somebody else's desk. Everybody laughed.

Shasta kept her eyes on the gray-green vinyl floor tiles. She didn't say anything.

"Hey, Shasta!" a boy called, standing up to make himself taller. "You learn to talk yet?"

Shasta said nothing. She tried to walk to her desk, but they were all on their feet now, they crowded around her like one big animal with too many blue-jeaned legs and a roaring, hurtful voice.

"Shasta disasta!"

"Say something, Shasta!"

"Nah, Shasta can't talk. She's a baby."

Why were they so mean? Why didn't the teacher make them stop, make them sit down, make them write five hundred times I Will Be Nice to Shasta? But the teacher didn't even look up. All she ever did was sit at the desk and correct papers.

"Shy Shasta! Shy-asta!"

"Let me alone," Shasta whispered.

They couldn't hear her, of course, but they saw. "Hey!" a boy yelled. "Her lips moved!"

"Shasta said something!"

They didn't bother to ask what she said. They never listened. They would just keep picking on her and picking on her like picking the edges off a sheet of notebook paper, they would keep picking her to bits until the bell rang, and nothing she could say would make a bit of difference—

"I said," bellowed a loud, commanding voice, "let me alone! Craven scoundrels! You're nothing but a rabble of dirty-necked, rascally *hooligans.*"

There was a breath of utter startled silence. Shasta saw kids standing with their mouths open in astonished ovals, their eyes wide, staring at her.

"Wh-*what?*" a boy stuttered.

"Look it up if you don't understand," the voice shot back. Shasta recognized that damp green voice. But what—how—she stood like her classmates with her mouth agape, and the voice was coming right out of her.

"Hooligans," it lectured. "Unruly, lackwit scaliwags. And you! There at the desk. You call yourself a teacher?"

Oh, no. Shocked, Shasta turned to see whether Mrs. Miller had heard.

"You're nothing but a sad excuse for a pencil pusher," the voice continued severely. "Pay attention! Teach these young people some manners, teach them compassion and consideration, *teach* if you're a teacher!"

At first Mrs. Miller was so absorbed in correcting her papers that she didn't notice that anyone was talking to her. But then her head jerked up and she looked at Shasta, her eyes round. "Excuse me?"

"I said—"

With a great effort Shasta managed to close her own mouth, pressing her lips tightly together. The voice went right on talking, but now it sounded muted and throaty.

"—a teachereachhhrrahemahhrrmmm—" Shasta found herself coughing. It felt like something was tickling the inside of her throat with long webby toes. She had never coughed so loud in her life. Behind her in the classroom she heard kids tittering.

"Frog in your throat, dear?" Mrs. Miller asked kindly.

Shasta just gawked.

"Exactly," the voice croaked.

But how could it be?

It just wasn't possible.

Shasta stumbled through math and social studies and health in a daze, with her mind going like a squirrel in a cage: That was a big frog.

It had taken both her hands to carry it. No way could it fit in her throat. No way. No. Not possible. Not happening.

In math, she forgot to hand in her homework. In social studies, she flunked a quiz. In health class, she could not remember what a larynx was. And then when she did remember, she spelled it "larinks." But she didn't think about the spelling until she got to English class.

She was going around with a frog in her larynx? That would explain where the frog had disappeared to. Maybe because it had no ribs it had managed to squeeze in somehow? Would it need to be surgically removed?

Or would they just have to leave it in there forever?

"Shasta, name the parts of speech," her English teacher was saying.

Oh. Oh, boogers, he was calling on her? Shasta sat with her mouth open. Could not think.

But she answered anyway. Or rather, the lumpy, tickly, green feeling in her throat answered for her. Loudly. "Nounsense," it declared, "pronounsense, verbosity, abject adversity, preposterous argumentation, and courtesy!"

Shasta knew that quacking voice. She'd know it anywhere. There was a frog in her throat, all right.

And it was saying such silly things that everybody was laughing at her, roaring with laughter. The teacher was laughing and clapping at the same time. Shasta tried clearing her throat—"Ahem, ahem, hrrmmm!"—then started to cough, trying to cough the frog out and get rid of it.

She coughed so hard that the teacher stopped laughing and peered at her. "Do you need to go see the nurse, Shasta?"

Shasta shook her head and coughed some more. "Shasta's just a disasta!" some kid yelled, and then the other kids laughed at her some more as she coughed and coughed. But it was no use coughing, even though the tickly feeling made her cough until her ribs ached. The frog was stuck tight in her throat with its feet dug in; she could feel it.

"Stop talking for me!" she whispered when she could speak.

"Then speak for yourself," the frog said out loud, and everybody looked at her like she had sprouted an extra head.

LUNCHTIME.

The morning had been so awful that Shasta felt worn out, almost relaxed, by the time she walked into the cafeteria. After all, things couldn't get much worse.

She had waited until the line was down, because kids always picked on her when she stood in line. So by the time she got her tray, all that was left was some sort of pre-chewed meat in yellow gravy. Lovely.

She carried her tray without dumping anything and sat at a table by herself, as usual. But right away kids came over to hassle her. "Shasta, you're just a disasta!" said a tall, redheaded girl. Only this time, she was smiling as she said it.

"Yeah," some boy said. "The way you yanked Mrs. Miller's chain, that was really cool."

Shasta blinked.

"What's a hooligan?" asked the redheaded girl.

Quickly, before the frog could answer for her, Shasta spoke up. "I didn't say that!" Anxiety made her voice loud enough so that they could hear her for once. "The frog said that. Ahem! See, I have this stupid frog in my throat and it, ahem! It talks. It snuck in while I was asleep because it wanted a wet place. It—"

The kids were laughing at her.

At first, Shasta wanted to crawl right under her lunch tray and hide. She felt like a puddle of yellow gravy on the floor. But then, all of a sudden, like seeing a star wink into light, she realized how funny it was. A frog? A talking frog, yet? In her throat? It was so silly, so goofy, so goosy-loosy ridiculous that she had to laugh, too. A burst of laughter tickled her throat and made her laugh some more. Laughing caught hold of her like coughing but a lot more fun. She threw back her head and yelped with laughter. She bellowed, she roared, she quacked and honked and gasped with laughter. Now the kids were laughing because she was laughing so hard, or maybe because they had never seen Shasta laugh before. They were laughing with her.

"RAH-ha-ha-ribbit!" Inside her, the frog was laughing, too. Shasta and the frog laughed twice as loud as anybody in the cafeteria.

Shasta laughed herself hoarse. Tears ran down her face. But she felt a lot better.

"Frogs like wet places," she declared, "and I am a wet place." She wiped her face with her hands.

"You're a swamp," somebody said.

"Yeah! I've got a frog in my throat and tadpoles in my belly, probably. I'm an ecosystem."

And after that, the day went great. Kids gathered around her and talked to her. She was the most interesting thing that had happened since school started. They still called her Shasta the disasta, but they were teasing, not picking on her.

It was so simple. All they wanted was for her to talk. And laugh.

After school, as Shasta was trying to sort out the mess in her locker, the redheaded girl came up to her. "So what does 'hooligan' mean, anyway?" she asked, smiling.

"I don't know." But Shasta didn't speak loudly enough to be heard over the hallway noise.

So the frog took over. "Look it up!" the frog barked.

"You're funny." The girl had a friendly smile.

THE NEXT MORNING, Shasta woke up early, took about half a second to think, then sat up in bed, eyes open wide, looking. Then she smiled. There was a big, lumpy bullfrog sitting in the middle of her bedroom floor.

"Hi," Shasta whispered.

"Louder," ordered the frog.

"*Hi!*"

"Much better." The frog's wide mouth turned up at the corners in a self-satisfied smirk. "Do you think you can handle those hooligans yourself now?"

"Yes." Shasta had spent two hours on the phone the night before with the red-haired girl, whose name was *Timothy*, of all things. Kids teased her about her name, she said. Shasta had a friend.

"Good. That notion you had of a frog in your throat, by the way, is patently absurd. It would be prohibitively dark and constrictive for any self-respecting frog to lodge in your throat."

"But if you weren't in my throat, how—"

"Nonsense. I feel most unpleasantly dry. Would you kindly take me outside?" the frog said in a commanding tone.

But Shasta didn't mind the frog's bossiness. She got herself moving and dressed quickly, feeling just plain good, and not only because her throat no longer felt swollen and lumpy and green. She felt good all over. As soon as she had her shoes on, she scooped up the frog and went thumping down the stairs. Passing through the kitchen on her way to the back door, she found her parents sitting at the table, each sipping coffee and reading a section of the newspaper. "Good morning, Mom," Shasta called. "Ahem! Good morning, Dad." Loudly enough to make them look at her.

Her mother glanced up, saw the frog, and her mouth dropped open; she seemed unable to speak.

"Where'd you get that?" demanded her father.

"I *told* you I had a frog in my throat." Shasta smiled and ran out the back door.

In the yard, she set the frog down and looked at it. On the grass, cobwebs sparkled with silver dew, and the frog sat wetly shining, greener than the clover, looking back at her with glistening golden eyes. Its eyes, so beautiful—Shasta had not noticed before.

"Well, Shasta, my princess," the frog said rather more softly than usual, "you got your wish. Just not the way you expected."

Shasta nodded.

"It's time for me to go," the frog said.

Shasta opened her mouth and spoke clearly. "Might I wish on a star again sometime?"

"Of course. And your wish will come true. Just be careful. Wishes are tricky."

The frog began to pale and disappear, like a star fading in daylight.

"Thank you, Godmother," Shasta whispered. Then she remembered, and said it out loud. "Thank you, Godmother."

Golden eyes smiled back at her before they winked and vanished into early-morning sunshine.

About the Authors

. . .

BRUCE COVILLE is a former teacher, gravedigger, and toy-maker who has written more than seventy books for young readers, including the international best-seller *My Teacher Is an Alien*. Among his other well-known titles are *Space Brat*; *Jeremy Thatcher, Dragon Hatcher*; and *Into the Land of the Unicorns*. As a kid he lived in a house with a back-yard that sloped down to a lovely swamp, a place that became one of his favorites. He now lives in Syracuse, New York, with his wife, Katherine (who has illustrated many of his books), as well as a varying number of strange children and adorable animals. He does not, at the moment, own any frogs.

ROBERT J. HARRIS is a Scot, an occasional fencer, and the in-ventor of the best-selling fantasy game Talisman. He has written more short stories than anyone else is interested in counting, and is currently working on his third novel (in case anyone is counting). He lives with his wife and three sons in a house that has no cats in it.

BRIAN JACQUES is the internationally loved author of the Red-wall series, now thirteen books strong and growing. A regular visitor to the *New York Times* Bestseller List, Redwall has found almost as many adult fans as those not yet out of their teens. The most recent addition to the series, *Lord Brocktree*, is being released by Philomel Books this autumn. Mr. Jacques began the series years ago in order to entertain the children at Liverpool's School for the Blind. A popular radio host and storyteller in his native Liverpool, Mr. Jacques is currently at work on his next novel. For more information, visit Mr. Jacques at his web site: www.redwall.org.

JANET TAYLOR LISLE has long had a fascination with the nature of reality. This fascination permeates her well-loved novels, among them *Forest*, *The Lampfish of Twill*, *The Great Dimpole Oak*, and *Afternoon of the Elves*, which received the Newbery Honor Medal in 1990. Her most recent title, *The Lost Flower Children*, was named one of the Best Books of 1999 by *School Library Journal*. She lives on the coast of Rhode Island, where her house overlooks a salt pond very much like Delia Broom's in her story here. For more information, visit Janet Taylor Lisle at her web site: www.janettaylorlisle.com.

DAVID LUBAR is a writer and video game designer who has spent an awful lot of time in the company of frogs. Besides penning froggy fiction from his pad in Pennsylvania, he also created the Game Boy version of Frogger. Last summer, in the throes of amphibian addiction, he and his daughter squandered many hours playing the Frog Bog game on the boardwalk at Wildwood, New Jersey. When he's not involved with frogs, he tries to give equal time to cats. If you liked his story, you can read more of his short fiction in *The Psychozone: Kidzilla and Other Tales*. His other books include *Hidden Talents*, *The Unwilling Witch*, and *Monster Road*.

STEPHEN MENICK is a familiar face in the Cairo bazaars, where last year he acquired a Middle Kingdom fragment of the Egyptian Book of the Dead and a fourth-century Greek copy of the last dictations of Pharaoh Ramses II. Mr. Menick's translation of the latter document is included in this book. Besides being a collector of antiquities, he is also the author of *The Muffin Child*, a novel of the Balkans. He resides near Washington, D.C., and is at work on yet another novel.

NANCY SPRINGER's interest in frogs began when she was a child, wandering the swamps along the Passaic River, and continued throughout her studies of fairy tales, folklore, and legends. She began writing fantasy for adults and children almost thirty years ago and hasn't quit yet. Her critically acclaimed novel *I am Mordred: A Tale from Camelot* was named an American Library Association Best Book for Young Adults and won the 1999 Carolyn W. Field Award. Its follow-up, *I am Morgan le Fay*, will be released by Philomel Books in the spring of 2001.

JANE YOLEN, author of more than 200 books and as many short stories for children and adults, has been called "America's Hans Christian Andersen." Her picture book *Owl Moon* received the Caldecott Medal in 1988, and she has won dozens of other awards, including the

Nebula, the World Fantasy Award, the Regina Medal, the Kerlan Award, and two honorary doctorates. She is married and has three children and three grandchildren. "Green Plague" is not her first story about frogs. She is the creator of the beloved Commander Toad books, the easy-reading fantasy science fiction series about frogs and toads in space, as well as the frog version of "The Emperor's New Clothes" called *King Long Shanks*.